# uses
# for
# boys

## erica lorraine scheidt

ST. MARTIN'S GRIFFIN
NEW YORK

This is a work of fiction. All of the characters, organizations, and events portrayed in this novel are either products of the author's imagination or are used fictitiously.

www.stmartins.com

ISBN 978-1-250-00711-7 (trade paperback)
ISBN 978-1-250-01381-1 (e-book)

First Edition: January 2013

10  9  8  7  6  5  4  3  2  1

*For my mom.*
*And for Jennifer and Sonja.*

# uses for boys

# the tell-me-again times

In the happy times, in the tell-me-again times, when I'm seven and there are no stepbrothers and it's before the stepfathers, my mom lets me sleep in her bed.

Her bed is a raft on the ocean. It's a cloud, a forest, a spaceship, a cocoon we share. I stretch out big as I can, a five-pointed star, and she bundles me back up in her arms. When I wake I'm tangled in her hair.

"Tell me again," I say and she tells me again how she wanted me more than anything.

"More than anything in the world," she says, "I wanted a little girl."

I'm her little girl. I measure my fingers against hers. I watch in the mirror as she brushes her hair. I look for myself in her features. I stare at her feet. Her toes, like my toes, are crooked and strangely long.

"You have my feet," I say.

In the tell-me-again times she looks down and places her bare foot next to mine. Our apartment is small and I can see the front door from where we stand.

"Tell me again," I say and she tells me how it was

before I came. What it was like when she was all alone. She had no mother, she says, she had no father. All she wanted was a little girl and that little girl is me.

"Now I have everything," she says and the side of her foot presses against the side of mine.

# eight is too big for stories

**B**ut everything changes and I'm not everything anymore. We're in the bathroom and she's getting ready.
His name is Thomas, she says, and he won't like it if she's
late. She tugs at the skin below her eyes, smooths her eye-
brow with the tip of her finger. I'm getting old, she says.

"Tell me again," I say.

"Eight is too big for stories," she tells me. She sweeps
past me to pick out a dress and when she does, I know. I
know this dress. It's the dress she wore the first time, the
dress she wore the last time she left me alone. It's yellow
and when I touch the fabric, my fingers leave marks.

"Stop that," my mom says and steps out of reach. Then
she sprays perfume between her breasts and I turn away.
I know what comes next. She'll go out and I'll get a
babysitter. She'll wear perfume and put on nylons. She'll
wear high-heeled shoes. The babysitter will sit at our
kitchen table and play solitaire.

"Why do you have to go?" I say.

"I'm tired of being alone," she says and I stare at the
wall of her room. The bathroom fan shuts off in the next

room. Alone is how our story starts. But then I came along and changed all that.

"You're not alone," I say. My back is to her and on the wall of her bedroom are the photographs I know by heart. The pictures that go with our story. She always starts with the littlest one. The one of her mother.

"The last one," my mom says, meaning it's the last picture taken before her mother died. She died before I was born. "She was so lonely," my mom says. Our story starts on the day that her father left her mother. It starts with my mom taking care of her mother when she was just a kid like me.

I can take care of you, I think. But already she has her coat on. She's opening the front door because Thomas is waiting downstairs.

I look at another photo, the one of me at the beach sorting seashells and seaweed and tiny bits of glass. In it, I'm concentrating and wearing my mom's sweater with the sleeves rolled up.

"Bye," she calls and I look up, but the door is already closed.

# he's our family now

She goes out that night. She goes out the next night. I sleep alone in her bed and when she comes home, she packs a suitcase. She's going away for the weekend, she says. She's going away for the week. In between she comes home. She repacks. She washes her nylons and hangs them in the shower. She washes her face in the sink. I watch her in the mirror as she gets ready to go out again. She looks at her face from different angles. She pinches and pulls at her skin.

Then I meet this man. This Thomas. She brings him home like he's some kind of gift.

And I'm told to be nice. I'm told to stand still. I'm made to wash my face.

I stand in front of him with my arms straight down at my sides. He's in the kitchen, crossing in front of the light like an eclipse. Our kitchen table looks strangely small. Our ceilings too low. I'm watching the front door and willing him to walk back out of it. Instead he bends down until his face is even with mine.

"She looks just like you," he says.

"You don't look like anyone special at all," I tell him. And I curse him. And I start a club to hate him. And I make a magic spell to get rid of him. And when she marries him, when we pack up our apartment and move into his house, when I change schools and have to eat the food he likes to eat, I don't talk to him.

"Anna," my mom says.

"What?" I say.

"Be nice," she says. "He's our family now."

# our story

The pictures stay packed away. I unpack my stuffed animals and line them up against the wall of my new room. I put the smaller ones in front so they can see. I tell them our story. I had no mother, I tell them. I had no father.

"Tell me again," they say.

# after the divorce

I sleep alone in my bed. I eat the food he likes to eat. I learn to be quiet and when he leaves, when he packs a suitcase and slams the door, I'm glad.

He moves out and we stay in his house, my mom and me.

"Now we have a house," she says and she says it more than once. She wanted a house, I think. And then I think, now we have a house. Now, I think, we'll be happy.

"A house is like a raft on the ocean," I tell her. And I tell her not to cry.

After the divorce, I think things will go back to how they used to be. A return to the tell-me-again times. After the divorce, I think, we'll unpack the photos and hang them on the wall. After the divorce, I tell her how good she looks. And she really does look lovely in a sad, made-up kind of way. She wears a lot of burnt orange and dark red, dark green. She lightens her hair and talks about getting a face-lift.

But her eyes go dreamy when I speak and she never really listens.

I'm nine years old. Look, I want to say, you are beautiful. But she hates being at home with me. Having a
child is another kind of defeat.


When she does get a face-lift, it's Armageddon—angry
cuts and shiny black stitches, a runny egg yolk of yellow-
blue bruises. Her mouth and eyes are swollen. I can't
even look at her. I won't speak to her.

In the bathroom, I run the water in the sink and look
at my face. I cross and uncross my eyes. I frown. I smile.
I close my eyes and open them really fast to catch myself. I'm her little girl. Arms spread. I'm her five-pointed
star.

All she wanted was a little girl and I'm that little girl.

"I can take care of you," I say. I say it out loud over
the sound of the water and then I say it again. My voice
is hoarse from not speaking for so long. I run into her
room to tell her. I forget and leave the water on. I burst
into her room.

"I can take care of you," I say.

But she needs quiet now, she says. The room is dark
and she turns her bandaged face away from me.

"Not now," she says. She needs to heal.

# waiting

Not now. The house is uneasy. Waiting. The worst part is that I'm alone. I watch a thin line of ants snaking through the kitchen. I put my face so close that my breath disrupts their path. They right themselves and keep on, winding along the wall and down the counter and back behind the refrigerator. I fill a pitcher of water and set it quietly on my mom's bedside table.

# after the face-lift

After the face-lift there's a new dress. There's a George and then a Martin. Martin prefers the blue dress, my mom says. The new dress. George likes the yellow. Then there's Robert.

"He's the marrying kind," she says.

She doesn't bring them home to meet me, these new ones. And when she marries Robert, she doesn't bring him home either. He's not a gift to me. My mom's new husband and her new face stretch tight against the bones of her old one.

"We're going to be a family," she says when she gets back from the honeymoon. She's standing in the bathroom with bobby pins in her mouth, arms over her head, arranging her hair.

"Wouldn't you like that, Anna?" she says. "A real family?" She's curling pieces of hair and then pinning them up. There's a slip over her bra and her new face is pale, waiting to be made up. She doesn't meet my eyes in the mirror. She's married a man with two sons, I learn. She goes on, curling, twisting, pinning.

"And you must be Anna," my mother's new husband says when we meet. "This is Anna," he says, turning to his sons.

"Hi," I say. They're bigger, older than me, hunched over in identical jackets. Sullen, acne-strewn boys who look warily at my mom and me. My mom is not a gift to them either.

The five of us move into a big house in the suburbs outside of Portland. A big new house with a big yard and tall glass windows.

"I always wanted a house like this," my mom says and she sighs and puts her arm over my shoulder. "This," she says, "is the house I always wanted."

# we're a family now

I don't want this house. I want to go back to the tell-me-again times when I slept in her bed and we were everything together. When I was everything to her. Everything she needed.

I unpack my stuffed animals and line them up against the wall of my new room. I put the baby ones in front so they can hear. I tell them our story. "I had no mother," I say. "I had no father." I was all alone and all I wanted was a little girl, I tell them. I pick a different one each time. "You," I tell a blue stuffed bear. "You are my little girl."

It's a deep Oregon summer and the sun fights its way into the yard through the dense pine. It's hot and every day I wear the same blue shorts and my favorite pair of sneakers. I cut my own bangs and my mom says they're crooked and half in my eyes. My room is upstairs, near her and the stepdad. The boys have their rooms downstairs.

"We're a family," my mom says. But we're not a family. We're something else.

# the stepbrother

I'm on the living room floor eating cereal and watching cartoons in a patch of morning sun. It's Saturday, but school's out anyway. I spill the milk and wipe it up with the hem of my T-shirt. I go back to the kitchen for another bowl. I don't even see it coming. A sharp crack and the tall glass window shakes like it's been slammed with a rock. The television is suddenly loud.

I'm out the door, racing around the side of the house. My sneakers skid against the bark dust. By the time I get there, the younger stepbrother is already crouched next to the injured bird. I look up at the window and see the reflection of trees, the faint smudge from its body where it sped headlong into the glass.

The stepbrother picks it up and cradles it in his hands. Cups it close to his chest. The shade makes patterns on his face. There are patterns all around us. I'm holding my breath and I can feel my heartbeat. I can see the tiny movements of the bird's chest. I'm hoping for something different. The stepbrother is hoping. We're holding our breath. The stepbrother is close enough to touch. It's the sweaty middle of day. I'm hoping so hard I can feel the throb of it in my ears.

When it dies the stepbrother looks down at his hands. He doesn't say anything, just drops the little body in the bark dust and walks back inside the house and locks the door to his room.

I follow him and stand at the top of the stairs listening. I think maybe I can hear him, but then it's like I don't hear anything.

In the bathroom I look at myself in the mirror. I don't look like my mom anymore. I don't look like anyone. I look at my reflection. This lying house tricks the birds. Why do we live in this lying house?

I hate this house.

The TV is still on and I walk around the empty upstairs. The TV is so loud I can hear it from under my bed where I keep a blanket and my favorite stuffed animals. I climb under and gather them around me.

"We're a family," I say and hold them tight.

# the dream

Nobody wants to be in the lying house. The step-brothers stay away. They go to their mother's. They stay with friends. Their rooms are empty. My mom and the stepdad leave early to go to work. They come home late. They come in after I'm supposed to be asleep. They lean and laugh in the hall, bumping into things. They speak too loudly.

My mom opens my door and asks why I left the TV on, why all the lights are on. Her voice is strange. Then she walks away leaving the door open and I hear them leaning and bumping in their room.

I have a dream and in it everyone in the world is racing to the same place on the globe. I can see the whole globe and the frantic racing. It's a buzzing, like the static of the television and it gets faster and louder until I wake up. I fall back to sleep, but later the dream returns.

"Stay home with me," I say to my mom. "I don't want to be alone." It's morning and I'm watching her get ready in the bathroom that smells like the stepfather.

"You're not alone," my mom says. She's thinking of

the stepbrothers. "And besides, you should make some friends. Don't you want to make friends?" And then she puts on her lipstick and blots it on a piece of toilet paper.

I want to tell her about the dream. Even awake I can hear the buzzing at the edges of things. I look down at my bare feet. Hers are already in stockings and heels. She steps past me.

"Have a good day," she says, leaving.

# summer

Summer stretches out and my mom redecorates. She hires men who tear out all the carpeting and replace it with unbroken expanses of beige. The stepdad pays for everything. She buys bedroom sets, a living room set, and one for the family room. Everything matches. She paints my room yellow and buys me a yellow dress to match. I'm almost ten. I hate yellow dresses.

The stepbrothers won't let her touch their rooms. They lock their doors. They shun us. I hang around the hallway hoping they'll talk to me. We have imaginary conversations. I hate all the same things they do. I make fake blood out of the berries on the Oregon grape outside their window and hope they'll notice my smudgy fingerprints on the light switches. But they're like spies. They enter the house through the side door, close the vents so I can't hear them talk, eat their meals after I've gone to sleep.

# fall

It's still hot when the school year starts. All the kids already know each other and I am too something for them. Too quiet or strange. Too sad, one girl says. I sit alone on the bus and stare out the window. I drag my backpack along the ground on the way home from the bus stop. I arrange my stuffed animals along the wall of my room, the little ones in front.

# winter

At first I don't notice when the stepfather stops coming home. By spring it's over.

# spring

**W**hy?" I ask my mom.

"Men leave," she says. "Just like my father," she says. "Just like yours."

# the big house

It's raining when the stepbrothers emerge from their rooms. The divorce is almost final and they're moving out. They wear a uniform of worn sneakers and faded green army coats and they drag their stuff out of their rooms in large green duffle bags. They walk right past me in the hall without saying a word. Then they're gone and it's strange to see their doors ajar. The carpet in their rooms doesn't match the rest of the house.

I poke around looking for signs of them, but there's only a pile of dirty clothes on the bathroom floor. My mom watches me and then sighs and goes back upstairs. This time there's no crying. She rearranges the furniture and spends long hours at her new job. The one she has to dress up for and travel for. The divorce is decided and we stay in the big house alone, my mom and me.

"It's such a beautiful house," she says.

# after the divorce

Everything changes.

My mom never goes downstairs. She doesn't mention the stepfather. She never mentions the stepbrothers. She comes home late and I don't know where she goes. She sprays her hair with hairspray and I stand in the doorway to the bathroom and watch. She sprays perfume on her neck and then leaves, turning off the light and stepping past me. I follow her around in my pajamas and she says, before she leaves, hurry up and get dressed. Then she takes her coat from the hall closet and a green leather briefcase that she leaves on a kitchen chair.

"Don't miss the bus," she says. But instead, I get in her bed and snuggle in the sheets. They still smell like her. I look at the picture of her mother that she hung back up on the wall. The one where her mother is looking at nothing, at something, in the distance.

"She's so alone," my mom always says when she looks at it.

I watch the minutes change on the alarm clock.

At 7:35, I get dressed and eat cereal in front of the TV.

I walk to the bus stop and stand near the other kids. When I come home after school I unlock the door with the key I keep in my backpack. I turn on the TV in the living room and leave it on through the after-school specials, through the evening news, through the shows I like to watch before I go to bed. I eat pizzas from the freezer and leave my dishes in the sink. Once a week the cleaning lady comes and she runs the dishwasher.

Sometimes I go downstairs and sit in the empty rooms. I can hear the TV from upstairs. I wonder where the stepbrothers are now.

# boys

My classroom looks out at the parking lot and there's nothing to see there.

"There's nothing to see out there, Anna," Ms. Wenderoth says and I turn to look straight ahead at the boy in front of me. Mark or Matt. Richard or Tom. Any boy. Some back-of-the-neck boy. Some Mark-Joe-Matt-Richard-Tom-Billy-Chris boy. Just a shoving-in-the-hall boy. A milk-through-his-nose boy. Just boys. Just there. Like teachers and desks and powdered soap in the girls' bathroom.

I'm thirteen and now I have a friend, Nancy Baxter. She sits in the front of the classroom. She doesn't care much for boys.

After school, at her house, Nancy's older sister offers to braid our hair if we sit still in front of the mirror. So we sit like that, Nancy and me, as still as we can, side by side in chairs facing the mirror in their pink bathroom, towels folded neatly on the rack behind us.

Nancy's sister is reflected in the mirror, looking at

herself, her hands automatically plaiting Nancy's thin blond hair. I can tell she doesn't need to concentrate, she knows Nancy that well. And they look alike, they have the same distracted, open-mouth gaze. Happy. Like it's so easy to be them. To be sisters. They don't even question it. Or the sound of their mom, moving around in the next room.

I want to be like Nancy is now, eyes closed, sister tugging at my hair. I close my eyes and pretend that I have a sister who can braid my hair without looking. That this is my family. My home. I lean my head back and feel hands pulling gently against my scalp.

I drift. Hands deft in my hair. My mom next to me. Our faces together in the mirror. I drift, but when I open my eyes again Nancy is looking at my reflection. Sometimes Nancy catches me doing this, caught up in wanting something she has and I don't even know why I do it. I just know that Nancy won't come to my house anymore. She says that it's weird that nobody is ever home. She told her mom and after that her mom called my mom and said she didn't want the girls playing alone anymore and from now on I could come to their house.

Nancy's sister is talking about boys but they're nothing like the boys in our school. They do things with the girls. Secret things. And Nancy's sister says she knows what to do with them. She knows what they're good for. I'm watching her talk and braid with her fingers and she's looking at herself like she's weighing her good features against her bad and talking about boys like Nancy and I know what she's talking about.

And then Nancy's mom comes in and says, "Shush, what are you telling these girls?" And Nancy runs out giggling and at first I don't follow, because her sister hasn't braided my hair yet, but then I do.

When Nancy's mom drops me off at my house, I use my key to let myself in. The porch light and one in the kitchen. Nancy's mom doesn't know that my mom is out because my mom and I leave lights on.

Or maybe she does, because she says, "Are you going to be alright, Anna?" And I say that I am.

But my mom doesn't come home that night. She calls, because it's important to call if you're not going to come home, she says, and she says that since I'm a big girl now, I can feed myself and put myself to bed. She always says that. I can hear a lot of voices in the background and I know that she forgets. She thinks each Charlie or James or Michael is unique. She forgets that the things she says about this one are the same as the things she said about that one. She believes that each one is the one and she says each name like it's the only man's name she's ever said. Tonight she says James like it's a magic word. She's going to stay with James, she says.

"OK," I say. And then I put the phone back in its cradle and walk around the house turning on the lights.

# on the bus

The next day, coming home on the bus, Desmond Dreyfus sits next to me. He's laughing with his friends and I'm not paying attention because when I don't go to Nancy's house I ride the bus to my house and I always sit alone. I'm looking out the window and wondering if there are still pizzas in the freezer. But then Desmond moves up to the seat next to me and sits really close so our thighs touch and he says my name quietly so only we can hear.

"Anna," he says. "You're so pretty," and he looks at me like it's the first time he's ever seen me.

Everything flushes warm  The sun slants through the bus windows in bright shards. One on my lap. One across his face. In my head, I'm telling Nancy the story of how it happened. I'm narrating the story of how Desmond Dreyfus sat next to me, how his brown hair fell into his eyes when he said I was pretty. I'm thinking about Nancy, and Desmond Dreyfus puts his hand on the outside of my shirt right over my breast and the thin

29

cotton bra that my mom bought for me. I'm surprised, but I don't say anything.

I think maybe he's making fun of me. My breasts are pointy and I don't think that's what they're supposed to look like. Nancy doesn't have pointy ones and hers are bigger and in the bathtub my rib bones jut out higher than my breasts and I don't think that's the way it's supposed to be. But now Desmond has his whole hand over me and the warmth of his hand is nice and I fit perfectly in his palm and he doesn't look like he's making fun of me. He looks serious. Even when he looks back at his friends, Carl Drier and Michael Cox, and I look too, they don't look like they're making fun of me.

I stop narrating and look out the window. I like the warmth of his hand and the way I fit in his palm and the way he's slowly spreading his fingers. We sit there, me looking out the window and him with his hand over my shirt, looking back at his friends. We sit there for what seems like a really long time. Then he lifts up the bottom of my T-shirt and puts his hand underneath against my bare skin. He covers my pointy breast with his palm, bra and all. It doesn't feel like anything I've ever felt before. I feel thirsty and now I can't look at Desmond or his friends, because his hand's under my shirt and I wonder if anyone else sees.

The bus slows down. It's my stop. "This is my stop," I say and my voice sounds strange. Desmond takes his hand away and I grab my backpack and Desmond says,

"Bye Anna," and the other kids turn around to look because they've never heard him say my name before.

"See you tomorrow," he calls.

But tomorrow Nancy doesn't have dance class, so we go to her house and we choreograph a dance to a song her sister likes and I spend all day waiting to tell her about Desmond's hand but then I don't.


At lunch the next day Desmond stops and says hello to Nancy and me.

"I didn't know you knew him," Nancy says and I flush. My face is warm. Now I'm the type of girl boys notice, I think. And I feel a little superior to Nancy then.

That afternoon it's raining and all the kids run from the front door of the school to the idling bus. I have my backpack over both shoulders and I'm wearing my best blue jacket and my favorite jeans that look like the jeans that all the other girls wear. Desmond gets on after me and stops in the aisle next to my seat. His hair's wet and in his eyes and I feel flushed and excited when he looks at me.

"Can I sit here?" he says and he doesn't wait for an answer but sits down next to me on the small seat and after him Michael Cox and Carl Drier fall into the seat in front of us.

I can picture what it's going to be like for me now, what it's going to be like, how he'll introduce me to his friends and how he'll invite me to parties at Lisa Jenner's house and how I'll invite Nancy along and when they ask who invited her, I'll say I did.

I know what I want and this is what I want.

Desmond moves my backpack to the floor, reaches under my jacket, untucks my shirt, pushes his hand up and cups my breast. His position is awkward and angled so he can fit his arm under my tight jacket. I don't expect this quickening, this feeling in my chest and I'm not sure if I like it. And I don't know what to do and it's a quickening like a tightening and I feel this incredible thirst like I need to drink water and it's strange because it's somehow tied to his hand and the way he's spreading his fingers.

With his left hand he takes my right one and places it on the front of his jeans. I think he's going to pull me into a hug, but he places my hand on the front of his jeans and—it's his penis—so I pull my hand away and he catches it again with his and laces our fingers together.

"It's OK, Anna," he says in a breath. His right hand is still cupping my breast. I have this feeling like when I was little and I looked at the stepfather's dirty magazines. This feeling that seems like thirst and I'm staring out the window trying to figure it out and I like the way my fingers are laced with his. I never thought he'd want to hold hands with me, so I didn't think about wanting to hold hands, but now I know it's exactly what I want.

Then he unlaces his fingers and pulls my hand back down on his jeans and covers my hand with his. It's his penis and he's pushing my hand against it with his.

I look up and Michael Cox and Carl Drier are watching. They're turned around in the seat ahead of us, their faces just inches from ours. Desmond pushes my hand rhythmically against the hard knot in his jeans and I'm surprised by the insistent pressure of it, the hard separateness of it under his jeans. Not like a body part, not like a limb or a bone, more like a small animal.

I can't even rehearse the story of it to tell Nancy Baxter because I know I will never tell Nancy Baxter and now Desmond's other hand is moving and twisting under my shirt and he's pushing on my breast so it hurts and then he makes a noise. His eyes are squeezed shut and he's making a sneezing face and then there's a wet spot on his jeans under my palm and he takes his hand out from under my shirt and for a second it's like a rush of something, like I miss having his hand there, but now there's a wet spot on his jeans and Michael Cox laughs like a bark and I pull my hand away and pick my backpack up off the floor and put it in my lap and wrap my arms around it.

When I get home and turn on all the lights, I picture Desmond in my house with me so I don't have to be alone. I have a conversation with him in my head and ask if he wants to eat pizza and if he wants to watch TV and in my imagination we spend a lot of time sitting on the couch together. I don't think about his penis or the wet spot or Michael Cox's bark of a laugh. All my favorite shows are on and I watch them in my pajamas and then when I go to bed, I fall asleep right away and I don't dream at all.

# joey

After the divorce, after the stepdad punches me on the arm and says, "Better luck next time," after my mom learns new ways to leave me alone, Desmond Dreyfus stops sitting next to me on the bus. It's so sudden I think maybe I imagined the whole thing.

When Desmond stops talking to me so does Nancy Baxter, and in the mornings before school, before the light is anything but a faint smudge outside my window, I put my hands under my pajama top and try to get the feeling back.

Waiting for the bus, I have long conversations in my head. I talk to Nancy. I tell her everything. I talk to Desmond. I tell him how it felt, his hand under my shirt. The exploding warmth. I tell Nancy how I feel, like something's been taken away. Stuff I know she'd never really understand anyway.

I ride the bus every day now. I wait in front of the school with my backpack at my feet and this new boy, Joey Sugimoto, stands next to me. He's from Seattle and wears jeans that hang on his hips. His arms are long and thin and he doesn't talk to anyone. He doesn't know any-one yet, I think, and I like the way he looks. But more than that, I like the way he looks at me.

And since Nancy Baxter won't speak to me anymore, since she won't look at me in the hall or sit next to me in class and since she whispers to the other girls about me, I take Joey home. He can't believe how big and empty my house is.

"Where's your mom?" he says.

I show him her bedroom with its matching bedspread and drapes. I show him the neat rows of her shoes.

"Where's your stepdad?"

I show him where the stepbrothers slept and the bal-cony where the older one smoked pot.

"Where are they now?"

I show him the room that used to be the family room.

"Where's your real dad?"

I show him what I look like without my shirt and how my bra attaches in the front. He spends a long time just holding and kissing my breasts, one by one, and saying, "Oh, oh, oh."

# joey's my family now

Nobody's ever home at my house. That's what Joey says. He comes over every day after school. He's better than TV. He's interested in everything. I show him my mom's jewelry. I show him the contents of our refrigerator, our cupboards, the vibrator in her bedside drawer.

We have a bowl of cereal and then I show him the magazines under my mom's bed. We sit together on the floor and pull out the heavy box the stepfather left behind: *Penthouse, Playboy, Hustler.* We're shoulder to shoulder against the wall. Joey's jeans have a wide hole in the knee and his brown, bony kneecap juts out. I put my hand in the hole, exploring the scarred surface of his kneecap with the lightest tips of my fingers. He lets me. I can reach down his baggy jeans and trace the barely haired calf all the way to his ankle, or go in the other direction to his thigh, down to his warm cotton underwear.

Joey chooses a magazine and opens it directly to the center. We unfold the picture. The centerfold's skin is a peachy golden-yellow and watching Joey I can see a tiny reflection of her in his eyes. She has one arm over her head and the knuckles of her hand just graze the bright blue water of a tropical pool. All of this I see in an instant: perfectly round breasts pointing out of the picture at Joey's bent face, shiny blue water, thick brown curls that cover her shoulders and peek out from behind her waist. She lies on the thin red sheet, eyes almost closed. Between long, curled eyelashes are slits of unnaturally green eyes. She has a small smile. Centerfold girl is happy to have us look at her.

We turn the page. Still on the red sheet, centerfold girl spreads her legs so that we can see the naked folds. She has only the tiniest mustache of hair, like a thin indicator, and with one pointy, painted fingernail she pulls at her skin so we can see the darker parts, like bruises. In another picture, Joey's finger traces the crack between two round butt cheeks. My hand still snakes under his jeans, but he's grown hard now, and my hand's stuck there, not sure if it should pull away.

Joey pushes me over and takes off my shirt, then my bra. He rubs himself against my leg. Beyond his shoulder centerfold girl has slipped to the floor to watch.

Joey's saying things, breathing heavily against the side of my face. I'm here, I imagine him saying. I'm here, I'm here, and it's true. Joey's here every day after school. He's my family now. Anything's worth this. And he teaches me things. He teaches me how to hold his penis at the base, tight in a fist, and move the skin up and down. He teaches me how to take it in my mouth without using my teeth. Joey is very experienced.

"I'm experienced in the ways of love," he tells me.

I take off my shirt. Joey takes off his and we rub our chests together. My breasts are small and pointy, but Joey thinks they're perfect. When he kisses me, I feel important. Like I'm everything to him. Sometimes everything happy bubbles up and I want to be chased around the house. I secretly want to run around outside in the cul-de-sac without my shirt on. I make jokes about Joey's body, his skinny legs and concave chest. About the little red hickies I leave on his skin. He holds my wrists, says I can only be cured by kisses. Or he scissors his legs between mine, trying to take off my pants.

"We'll just lie together," he says.

I'm dizzy with his kisses. At my house it's empty room after empty room and we kiss in every one. It's like all I know are his lips. He has thousands of dizzying lips. I take off my pants and he rubs his penis against me, but I keep my legs tight together. Joey whispers in my ear and strokes my forehead like I'm ill. Everything is a negotiation. Everything moves in a series of degrees.

"Just a little, just a bit, just the head."

Day after day, hour after hour.

"If you love me," he says.

"If you care about me," he says.

"It's not fair," he says.

"I love you," he says. And I love you, I love you, I love you.

"OK," I say, but not because of that. Not because of what he says or how he says it. Not because I'm tired of waiting, or because I think I should or shouldn't, or that it's right or wrong—but because I want to. I like the way he makes me feel. I want to feel him. I want to feel him like that.

I say OK and we do. And it's not that much different than anything else we do.

# i belong here

Once we find this way of fitting together, I set about finding other ways. The back of my knuckles cup the hollow beneath his arm. My nose, my face, I could fit whole armies of things in this cavity, or just my cheek, my breast.

"What are you doing?"

I angle my body, arm outstretched, and stuff my right breast into the warm depression under his arm. His ribs press against mine. I penetrate him with my breast. We're boob fucking. It's awkward and mysterious. Fulfilling.

I rest my face against the bottom of his ribs and breathe into his narrow stomach. The skin stretches thin across his belly. There's an uncomfortable pucker to his belly button and I put my fingers in it, pulling at the lip, until I notice the black dirt inside.

My hand goes lower. The only lushness on his body is the bed of hair where his penis rests. I rest my cheek against his belly, turn away so he can't see my face. I have this view of him: down his belly to the wrinkled sheets between his legs. This view: his bumpy knees and out-turned feet.

We come unattached and I blow my cheek up full of air against his stomach. Again, double time, like a heart-beat.

On Fridays, my mom leaves a twenty-dollar bill and a note on the kitchen table.

"Rinse the dishes before you put them in the dish-washer," it says.

Joey and I have sex in her bedroom. He brings rub-bers that he steals from his brother and brags about how he can put them on with one hand. I like the way he looks at me with his eyes mostly closed and the way he kisses, like he's breathing in my mouth. Afterward we watch the gray sky darken behind heavy pine trees and listen to nothing at all. It rains silently on the house.

I'm fourteen. I go to school. I dress the way all the other kids dress. I wear my Levi's with expensive twill shirts. I wear the right tennis shoes, the white leather ones with the green stripes. But the outfit buys me noth-ing. Everyone has heard how I let Desmond Dreyfus feel around under my shirt while Carl Drier and Michael Cox watched. Everyone knows about Joey. The boys make V signs when they look at me and tongue the crack between their fingers. The girls call me a slut.

Joey lives in a thin-walled apartment at the bottom of

the hill near the freeway. His mom works and his dad, like mine, is gone. His brother drinks beer and watches daytime television. He asks if we're fucking and then kicks us out. We go back to my house. Joey loves my big clean house.

He loves the way it smells on Wednesday after the cleaning lady leaves and there are lines in the carpet from her vacuum cleaner. He takes deep breaths through his nose and leads me around, inspecting her work. Some-times, when she's still there after we get home from school, Joey talks to her, and she gives me a look. I'm too young to have boys over she thinks, but she won't say anything. She piles her worn leather purse and heavy coat on our kitchen table and before she leaves she col-lects my mom's check from the table in the entry hall.

Joey and I take the bus home together after school. We sit close together. No one talks to us. Nancy Baxter stares at me and whispers to her friends and I stare back at them until they look away. Nancy Baxter. It's hard to remember there was a time when she wasn't staring and whispering. Joey holds my hand. He doesn't notice the stares. All they see when they look at him is his no-name jeans, his worn shirts, the dirty Skoal cap he wears. Joey changed everything for me, I want to tell her. I'm not alone. The place where my hand fits in his, that place, that feeling? I belong there.

I hate Nancy Baxter. I hate the school bus.

We get off on the corner of a tree-lined street near

my house and it's raining but the sun is shining and it's so bright I have to squint. Joey stops, right there at the bus stop, and kisses me. He likes to put his hand up under my shirt and shock the adults driving by. The other kids scatter slowly toward their own houses until it's just Joey and me and the cars are going so fast that we're not shocking anyone.

The closer we get to my house, the quieter it is. There's no traffic here and the houses are locked, windows dark. I take Joey's hand in mine. His fingers are cold. He stops and looks at me intently like he's going to say something. His cheeks are wet from the rain, like he's been crying, and I realize that I must look like that too.

I keep the key to my house in my book bag and have to put it down while I unlock the lock and the dead bolt and when we get into the entry hall we're really careful. We take off our shoes and our jackets because my mom likes a clean house and she doesn't know about Joey.

In the kitchen we decide between cereal and frozen pizza. Some days we choose the pizza, which takes longer, but today we have cereal and Joey says I use too much milk. Afterward he wants to kiss me in the kitchen and take off my shirt and kiss my chest and I always feel kind of funny here because someone could see me if they were looking through the kitchen window.

"You're so beautiful," Joey says. And we kiss and kiss and our hands run up and down each other's backs and soon he leads me to my bedroom and I lie down on the bed. Joey likes to sit next to me, unzip my pants and help me pull them down. He likes to watch the way his trailing fingers make goose bumps on my skin. He likes to stroke my hair and put one hand over my eyes so I can't see what he's doing.

He covers my eyes with his hand.

"I'm moving back to Seattle," he says. "To live with my dad."

And then he doesn't say anything. He doesn't say he'll miss me or that he's sorry. Does he know he's leaving me? That I'll have to ride the bus home alone and come home alone and be home alone? They leave, I think, just like my mom says.

In the tell-me-again times, when I was seven, before the stepfathers and the stepbrothers, before the big house in the suburbs with its big windows and land-scaped yard, before Nancy Baxter and Desmond Drey-fus, when my mom and I lived in a little apartment in a little building downtown, I slept in her bed. It was a raft on the ocean, a cloud, a forest, a spaceship, a cocoon that we shared. I could stretch out like a five-pointed star and then she'd bundle me back up in her arms. I'd wake in the morning tangled in her hair.

Sometimes I want to be back there so bad I can't breathe. I can't close my eyes tight enough. I can't wish hard enough. Joey's hand is still over my eyes and I can feel the weight of him sitting next to me. I hear a sharp crack from somewhere in the house, like a bird flying headlong into glass, and I'm really cold all of a sudden and topless and my pants are down around my ankles. I push away his hand so I can cover myself up with the blankets. I'm fourteen and I hate Joey Sugimoto. I hate my bed. I hate this house.

I have to get out of here, I think.

The sun is still bright through the windows and making little rainbows against the rain. Joey's taking off his pants because he thinks we're going to have sex. I turn away from him and curl up into a little ball.

"Anna?" he says, but I don't say anything. After we have sex and it's dark out, Joey leaves like he always does. That night, when my mom comes home, she opens my door and sticks her head into my room.

"Good night honey," she says.

# after joey

Joey moves away. It's getting warmer and my mom has set the sprinklers to turn on automatically. They beat against the window when the sun rises and I wake early. In the bath I run my hands over my breasts, my stomach. I pretend they're Joey's hands.

The house gapes. My key echoes in the lock. I wear his Skoal cap to school but someone grabs it off my head in the hall and I can't get it back. I turn fifteen. We get a new cleaning lady. It's spring, but without Joey the school year lumbers on. I'm waiting for something to happen.

# alone

I decide to move downstairs into the stepbrother's room. The younger one's. It's dark and colder than the rest of the house. The windows are level with the ground outside. I carry everything I need in one trip. Sheets, a blanket, towels for the bathroom. A pillow from my bed. A French magazine I found at the thrift store. I'm wearing the jeans the stepbrother left behind and my hair's grown long again and tucks behind my ears. I go through a box of my mom's and find a photo of her when she was my age. She looks serious and sad and I pin the picture to the wall near the bed and try to imagine what she was thinking. Her life when she was fourteen: her father leaving, her mom retreating. Does she remember? I pin my hair like hers and lay back on the bed. I take the picture down and hold it close to my face.

When I visit the upstairs I feel like an explorer. I live downstairs now. A different life. A different person. My mom never comes down. She stands at the top of the stairs.

"I'm leaving," she calls.

# the dream

skip school and wander from room to room. I watch daytime TV. I make up illnesses and forge my mom's name to the bottom of notes. "Please excuse my daughter's absences this week," they say. "She had the stomach flu." Or food poisoning. Or an infection. I'm very careful. Nobody ever asks.

I stare out the window at a bit of bark dust and brush. I stare at the base of a fir tree and at the neighbor's fence and I think about our little apartment in the city. My mom's blue bedroom. Her warm sheets. At night I have the same dream. I dream that all the people in the world are racing to a single point on the earth, and when I wake up, the buzzing makes me feel like I have to get out of my head. But there's nowhere else to go.

My social studies teacher, Mr. Carlson, pulls me aside on the last day of school. He was my homeroom teacher too and he knew Joey. Once he gave us a ride home from school when we missed the bus.

"Are you OK, Anna?" he says. He's looking at me in a way I don't expect, like he wants to know more, and the kids, the kids I've gone to school with since grade school, push past me in the halls. Nancy Baxter's yellow ponytail turns a corner.

I'm not coming back to school. I've already decided. I'm supposed to go to the high school across the street next year. But I can't picture it. Maybe that's the problem, I think, looking at Mr. Carlson's beard. I can't picture anything.

Some other kid is waiting to talk to Mr. Carlson. "See you," I say and no one else talks to me as I leave the building and wait for the bus.

# nippery slipple

ive days later, on the day they're supposed to leave for vacation, I come upstairs and find my mom and her boyfriend standing in the entry. It's early afternoon and I'm wearing the stepbrother's T-shirt with a pair of cutoffs.

"Why are you still here?" I ask, crossing past them toward the kitchen. My mom is looking in her purse.

"I'm not going to have you just moping around," she says without looking up. And she tells me to get ready. "You're going with us," she says.


The resort is hot and sticky and full of families from Portland. I carry a stack of magazines to the pool and lean back into the sun. I drift. The whole place splashes and screams around me. I'm sun-stoned and dreamy when Delmi, a girl who was a year ahead of me in middle school, waves herself over and sits down. She reaches past me to the pile of pictures I've torn out of magazines. She flips through them, pulling out a picture of a tall girl in faded jeans stretched out in the sun.

"I like this one," Delmi says. She's wearing a thin green bikini and her family owns a house here so she knows everyone, but she seems just as happy to sit with me and look at pictures, one hand shielding her eyes from the sun.

"How long are you here?" she asks. And she asks if I want to come to a party at her house tonight. "Everyone will be there," she says. "Him," she points at a boy across the pool. "Her," she points at one of the lifeguards. "They'll be there," she says.

"Sure," I say and we look at another magazine.

Delmi's parents have a collection of schnapps that glisten like lacquer. Peppermint, blackberry, sour apple. I choose butterscotch and Delmi makes me a drink called a Slippery Nipple. Her stepbrother Todd calls it a Nippery Slipple. He sits down next to me on the bar stool in Delmi's parents' basement. We're waiting for the party to start.

He leans over and says it with his mouth tight against my ear.

"Nippery Slipple," and his breath is hot and there's the pressure of his chest against my arm. He pinches the tip of my breast and repeats it like it's my name, Nippery Slipple.

Delmi makes the drink. She reaches for the bottle, pours, and puts it back on the shelf. She's wearing a soft blue T-shirt that falls off her shoulder and then when she reaches for the Baileys it slips back. She turns around to look at Todd leaning against me.

"Leave her alone," she says and then she gives me my drink. "Ignore him," she says to me.

"I am."

"You're not," he says, reaching for my nipple again.

"I am," I say, but I can still feel the ghost heat of his breath against my ear. He's older than me, I think, out of high school at least. But not as old as Delmi's boyfriend who's twenty-two.

And very intelligent, she says.

I finish my drink. Todd disappears upstairs and I'm trying to think of a way to ask Delmi about him. Instead I ask for another drink. "Make me another drink?" I say.

"He's an asshole," she says. "I don't know why he's here. Usually he stays with his dad." Delmi lives with her dad and Todd's mom. They're gone all the time, she says.

I'm looking at Delmi, but thinking about Todd. I can see myself in the mirror behind the bar and if I dip my chin down, my hair falls in my eyes and I look sexy, I think.

I finish my drink and the basement fills with kids. Delmi's gone and Todd hasn't come back. I make my own Nippery Slipple.

I'm wearing my favorite red canvas shorts with a fluttery Egyptian top. Girls show up in summer dresses mostly or jeans and T-shirts with eagle wing jewelry. This summer all the girls wear eagle wing jewelry. The boys hunch together in groups. I spill my drink and make another.

Then Todd's back and I'm on the couch and he pinches my nipple again like he can and I flip him off, like I'm saying fuck off, this happens to me all the time. I lean back and drink my drink. I look older, I think. Somebody moves off the couch so he can sit next to me. I want to tell him things. I want to tell him about my mom. Why? But I do. I'm full of sympathy for my mom. I drink my drink. I have no mom, I say. I don't even care if it makes sense.

Then he says something about fucking. Fucking, I think he says. What's he asking? Have I ever fucked a boy? I dip my chin down and look up at him through my bangs. I try to look experienced. I make a joke and start laughing so hard I spit. What's so funny? I talk about love. I loved Joey, I say, and he left. Love wears off like the gold plating on eagle wing jewelry.

But I'm not sure what he's asking.

"I'm very experienced in the ways of love," I say. I can't stop laughing. The schnapps pours a thick blanket over my brain and Todd puts on dark sunglasses so I can't see his eyes. The kids next to us on the couch are making out and someone has turned off most of the lights. I'm pressed up against the armrest and Todd lays his head against the back of the couch like he's asleep. I can't even tell if his eyes are open.

Then Delmi's here again and her boyfriend's standing behind her with his arms around her waist. "Are you alright, Anna?" she says and I wave her off. I look over at Todd, but he's not there anymore and the couple's gone too, so I'm alone on the couch and it takes me a long time to get up and find my way down the hall to an empty room. It's a guest bedroom with a twin bed pushed up against the wall. I kneel down on the spinning bed and hug a pillow against my chest. The music is thumping from the other room and the bed won't stop its spinning.

I'm going to throw up.

I push myself up and make it to a garbage can by the door. Afterward I lie on the floor for a while.

Delmi comes in. "Oh, Anna," she says like maybe she's angry but then she helps me to the bed and I take off my shorts and climb under the thin blanket. She pulls the covers up under my chin and rests her hand on my forehead.

"I'm sorry," I say but I'm not sure if she hears me.

"Good night," she says from the doorway, then her boyfriend calls from the other room and she's gone. "I thought Todd left," I hear her say from a long way away and then I think she says my name but the bed is spinning again and I have to concentrate on my breathing. I open my eyes in the darkness and focus: in and out, in and out.

Now Todd's here, sitting by the side of the bed. His hand is on my arm. Then Delmi's back, shooing him out. "Leave her alone, Todd," she says.

Later he's back. My head sticks out from the blanket. I fight against the spinning bed. His profile in the darkness. My shirt bunches around me.

He pulls down the covers and I laugh. But he tugs at my shirt and pinches my bare nipple. Hard. I cover my chest.

He climbs on the bed.

I make noises. "Stop." I'm trying to locate him in the darkness. It's as though I didn't say anything.

Delmi, I think. She'll make it stop.

"Delmi," I say but it's less than a squeak. My heart beats in my ears. I can't hear him. I can't see him in the darkness. I can't remember what he looks like. His hands are like attacks. I say things but even I can't hear what I'm saying and finally I push hard against his arm so he knows I'm here. "Stop," I say. "It's me," I say. I want him to see me. He pushes harder and something rips and I feel a burning. I stop moving. I'm so still. I'm so still. Only the thumping in my ears.

I think he might care what I want but he doesn't.

He pulls down my underwear and pushes my legs open, holds them with his knees. My knee is screaming. He's digging into my thighs and I'm twisted and he's pulling my nipple and everything hurts and then suddenly he lets go. He puts on a condom and then he covers my mouth with one sweaty hand. Why? I wasn't even saying anything.

He pulls at my thighs. He pushes. He fits himself inside me. His knuckles between my legs. All of his weight on my knee. It's going to break. I hold my breath. All I can hear is his breathing and my heartbeat and then suddenly he stops.

I pull my arms away and cover my ears so I don't have to hear his ragged breath. I close my eyes so tight it hurts. He takes his hand off my mouth and wipes himself on the sheet. I think he's going to kiss me but I have vomit on my face. He doesn't. He's going to say something. My eyes are closed but I loosen my hands over my ears. He pushes off the bed and stands up.

"Don't tell anyone," he says.

# secret

I'm in the hot backseat, driving back to Portland with my mom and her boyfriend. The boyfriend's driving and the back of his head curves over the front seat like a rising planet. He has a full head of hair. The first stepfather was balding and the second, thinning, so, in terms of hair, my mom's moving up. Her own hair keeps getting lighter. It's so blond now, I can see right through it.

The boyfriend turns on the radio and sings along. He has a terrible voice. Even my mom rolls her eyes. I tap her on the shoulder and point at the sign to EATZ CAFE. I have to go to the bathroom. The boyfriend's hungry too, he says, and we pull over.

I'm wearing the same shorts as the night at Delmi's, but with a baggy T-shirt and moccasins. I wear the moccasins every day now. There's a bruise on my thigh that the shorts don't cover. I didn't tell Delmi.

"Did he come back?" she said when I saw her the next morning.

"He tried to kiss me," I started and already I'm telling

the story and it's changing in the telling. In this version he liked me.

But she's not listening and I never have a chance to tell the story, even to myself. And so I don't tell anyone. I want Todd to know that. And then I am telling it to myself. And in this version it's our secret.

There's a line for the bathroom and I'm behind a fat woman in shorts and dirty flip-flops. She tugs at her ponytail with one hand and holds her son by the neck with the other. She watches herself in the mirror. We're all looking at ourselves, lined up in front of the mirror. Ahead of her is a girl, younger than me and beautiful. Innocent. I look at her, still thinking about Todd. Her long, long hair is braided in two dark braids. The room smells of urine and lemon cleaner. There's a high window where flies enter and exit and for a long time the line hardly moves at all.

Back in the parking lot the sun glances off of the gas pumps and the E in EATZ. Cars flare and spark and I have to squint to make out my mom, leaning back against the headrest in the front seat of our car. The window flashes to obscure her then, as I get closer, frames her. She opens the door as I approach.

"Oh Anna," she says. "I hate this drive." She wears a lot of makeup, my mom, and sometimes it's all I can see when I look at her. There are little cracks in the surface under her eyes and a greasy line of shadow in the fold of her eyelid.

There was this boy, I want to say. I want to tell her about Todd and I want her to fold me up in her arms. I want her to know. But I don't tell her. I don't know which story to tell.

She looks at me. I'm standing right in front of her, in the open car door, with my eyes telling her what happened. I'm looking directly at her and my eyes are telling her everything. How he pulled down the blanket and pulled down the sheet. What happened after. How I waited there until morning, my knees pressed against the wall, listening. Wondering if he was going to come back. She looks right at me with all of her attention. Her eyes open wide and then narrow again. The blush and the mascara and the powder all soften together.

"How is the bathroom," she says. "Is it clean?"

# toy

**W**hen we get back to the suburbs, I cut the arms off my twill shirts and wear them over the T-shirt that the stepbrother left behind. I cut my own bangs. I spend a long time looking at myself in the mirror in the downstairs bathroom. It's windowless and dark and the fluorescent lights make heavy shadows under my eyes. If Joey were still here he'd put his face next to mine, his cheek against my cheek and meet my eyes in the reflection. I listen for the garage door, but my mom doesn't come home. She leaves for two days with a note on the table. Then she comes back. Then she leaves for a week.

I go to Goodwill. It's the size of a hospital, brightly lit and nearly empty. I'm wearing the stepbrother's jeans rolled up and Converse. A tight plaid shirt from when I was little. I'm looking for something. The perfect clothes. A uniform for the girl I want to be. I run my hands over the racks and then move to the far corner of the store. I'm methodical. Kids' clothes first, looking for shrunken blazers and thin faded T-shirts. Then to women's. Leotards, vintage bathing suits, high-waisted shorts. I try things on in the aisles. I look in the mirror and imagine. Am I this girl? Am I this one? I look through the scarves. Buckets of silky ones and chiffon ones. I'm looking for the tourist ones, the monuments of Washington, D.C. or the Leaning Tower of Pisa.

I find a T-shirt from the Mystery Spot. I find a scarf from the rock of Gibraltar. I'm hesitating over a pair of clogs when I see them. Perfect and perfectly small brown wingtips. Men's, but they look small enough to fit.

I put the clogs down and step forward. There's a girl my age hunched over like she's too tall or the light is too bright, wearing a long black dress from the seventies with a T-shirt underneath and she's walking right over to the shoes. She picks one up and looks down at it in her hands.

I don't think she sees me. There's music playing over the loudspeaker and an employee nearby straightening sweaters. I'm standing in front of the clogs and holding my T-shirt and scarf in one hand.

And then she says, "They're too small for me," like she knows I'm there. Like she sees me. I take a step closer but I don't say anything. She stares at the shoe in her hand.

I look at her and I look at the shoe. I look down at the floor and then I look around. "They might fit me," I say quietly.

The girl holds out the shoe. I step closer again and rest the T-shirt and scarf on a shelf. I take the shoe from her and turn it over in my hand. She's still looking at the ground, but I can tell her eyes are looking around. She has a narrow face. Narrow eyes. Her dress is thin and stretchy and I can see her hip bones. Her breasts are even smaller than mine. She's wearing high-heeled sandals and her hair is thick and long and straight like a child's. She's beautiful. She's beautiful and I want to know her.

Toy tells me every great thing she's ever found at Goodwill. She tells me about this dress, the black dress and the other dresses, a rainbow of dresses that she's found here. She looks at the ground when she talks and her eyes slant and dart over to mine and then back. I sit down on a bench and take off my sneakers. The wing-tips fit and they're perfect. I look at Toy and Toy's looking at my feet and she says it too. Perfect. Just like that.

"They're perfect," she says and then she sits down and takes my scarf off the shelf in front of us.

"I saw this," she says. "I wish I'd taken it." She's holding it up to the light and the gray cliff of Gibraltar is neatly in the center. "It's cool," she says.

I reach for the coveted scarf. "I'll loan it to you," I say and I hold my feet out in front of me admiring the shoes.

Toy and I shop together. There are a pair of sailor pants with a boy's name embroidered on the inside. There's a bright blue mohair cardigan. We stand in front of the mirror and try things on. I dip my chin so my bangs fall forward and I look at her eyes in the mirror but she looks only at herself. She puts a dress on over the one she's wearing, twists her hair up and holds it on top of her head. The she turns to me.

"What do you think," she says. And then she says, "My boyfriend would love this." And she emphasizes the word, love. "He would love this," she says. And she emphasizes the word, boyfriend. "My boyfriend," she says.

I look at myself in the mirror and dip my chin. She has a boyfriend, I think.

After we had sex the first time, Joey took the condom off and placed it next to the bed. "I'm your boyfriend now, you know," he'd said and when he said that, I made fists and filled his armpits. Stretched out the fingers of my hand and compared them to his. I think about Todd. His hand over my mouth. Toy turns around in the mirror.

"He would love this," she says again, pulling the short black dress off again.

In the end I let her buy the scarf and she buys the short black dress and I buy the wingtips and the sailor pants and the T-shirt from the Mystery Spot. We each buy a few old *Vogue* magazines. We stand on the sidewalk and I hold our bags while Toy reapplies her lipstick. She does it without a mirror and when she's done, she looks up at the pregnant sky, heavy with clouds. I'm holding her bag in my hand and feeling like she could just walk away at any second and nothing will have changed.

I need something to change. I look up at the sky and try to figure out what to say. Toy stretches and then yawns.

"Let's go to my house," she says. And then she takes her bag and walks toward the bus stop.

# best friends

The bus winds through the city and out to Toy's neighborhood on the other side of the suburb from mine. She's talking about her family.

"From daughter to wife," is how she describes her mom, as if repeating something she'd heard. "He left us" is how she describes her dad. "The stepfathers," she says, "aren't worth describing."

"From stepfather to stepfather," I say.

"Me too," she says. And now her father has new kids. "Better kids," she says. "His finally-got-it-right family."

I stare at her profile.

"I'm the fucked-up daughter with the fucked-up mother," she says. "A leftover from his practice family."

My arms circle the bag on my lap. Toy has a story about everyone. I never met my dad. I don't know if he has another family.

Toy's father takes her to dinner once a month. The first Saturday of every month. As seldom as possible. "He hates to even look at me," she says. "I remind him

of my mom." She pauses, lifting her chin. "She's beautiful," she says.

Her dad, she says, takes her out and watches her eat.
He asks her about school. Then takes her home. He pulls
away from the curb before she gets to the front door.

Toy lives on a cul-de-sac just like I do and her house
looks like my house, except all the furniture is white, all
the mirrors have gold frames and her mom is home.

We're the same age, we slump the same way in all our
school pictures, have endured all of the same hairstyles.
There are empty rooms that the stepfather and stepbrother left behind, just like at my house. We could
switch places, I think, like in a movie. She's still talking
and I stare at her thin ankles, her scuffed shoes. Toy
looks like me in that way where she doesn't at all. Not
on the outside.


Everything changes. First there was my mom and then
there was Joey and now there's Toy and in this story I'm
not alone. She lets me curl her hair around my fingers.
She lets me wear her favorite shirt and roll up the sleeves.

She says it first. "You're my best friend," she says and
I feel something when she says it. I feel it in the tip of
my fingers, under my fingernails and in the palms of my
hand. I feel something so strong and so familiar that I
want to take it home and show my mom. See, I want to

say. I want to hold out my hands and show my mom so she can see it and remember.

I sit on the side of the tub and watch Toy get ready. She twists her hair up and catches it on top of her head. She curls her eyelashes, tints her cheeks. Pieces of dark hair escape from her barrette. I look at my own reflection, jagged hair and blue eyes. I want to be Toy. I want to climb into her and feel the ticking spiral of her thoughts in my head. But more than that, I want her to feel it too. I want her to want to be me.

# toy's story

It's late afternoon and we're sitting on the weathered lounge chairs in her mother's backyard next to an empty pool.

"After the divorce," she says. After the divorce their pool was emptied and never refilled. I'm flipping through an old *Vogue* and pointing out things I would wear and things I never would.

But back when the pool was full, Toy's saying, before the divorce, Toy's stepbrother had a party and Seth was there. "That was it," Toy says. "Right away I knew," and she stares off into the rhododendrons. Toy's my best friend now and we wear each other's clothes. We memorize the bus schedule between her house and mine. Seth, I know, is her boyfriend. I've never met him. He's older and a friend of Toy's stepbrother.

That reminds me. "What do you call a stepbrother after the divorce?" I ask. I think there should be a name for this.

Toy ignores me. "He had the greenest eyes you ever saw," she says. Her sentences always turn up at the end.

There was chemistry between them, she says, and chemistry, I'm made to understand, is crucial. "It's about how you smell. Not how you smell smell, but how you smell to him." She's looking right at me to make sure I understand, so I smell myself and lift my shoulders in a shrug.

I'm wearing oversized shorts and a thin white T-shirt. I wear my brown wingtips without socks. I rub my hands over my calves. It really isn't all that warm and when a cloud passes in front of the sun, it isn't warm at all. I pull a denim jacket over my chest.

"Everyone else ignored me," she says. "But Seth came right up and put his nose against my neck and said that I smell good." He was always smelling her, she says. She was a virgin when they met and now she says the best thing about sex is all the sniffing and smelling. I think she must be joking about that.

"He said you smell good?" I ask. I know when to ask a question or repeat what she says because she pauses, looks out at the rhododendrons and sighs. The day after they met he picked her up in his car and took her to his apartment. She wore her favorite dress, the one with the thin brown-and-green stripes, and a denim jacket.

"That jacket," she says, pointing to the one I've pulled over me. She'd taken a shower and shaved her legs and shaved under her arms and scrubbed between her legs, so she was cleaner than clean. But all he wanted to do was play music and read to her, smell the part of her neck under her chin and put his hands up under her hair.

70

"He didn't even want to kiss," she says. He liked it, she says, when she smelled him. So she leaned in, first behind his ear and then against the soft cotton of his T-shirt. She laid her cheek against his chest and waited, bent and awkward on the low couch. They laced their fingers together.

She stops talking, looks out at the rhododendrons and sighs. But I don't know what to say. I stare at the brown and rotting blooms.

"Did he smell good?" I ask. They had many dates like that. Sitting quietly together and smelling each other. She was falling in love, Toy says, and this is what it's like. Every morning she showered, shaved and was ready. Just in case. Ready for her first time.

"I was ready," she says.

I think about Joey. It wasn't like that. It happened in degrees. But I found that once you did those things with a boy there was no going back.

"What do you mean, no going back?" she asks.

"You know, to sniffing," I say, but she doesn't think that's funny.

Toy's mom comes out through the sliding glass door and I know she's been sleeping because her eyes are puffy and there are pillow lines on her face. She isn't anything like my mom who never sleeps in the daytime. She asks if we're hungry and then goes inside to get a twenty-dollar bill for pizza. They eat a lot of pizza.

Seth wanted the first time to be special. They spent

long afternoons talking about it and he whispered a litany of all the things he'd do to her and all the things she'd feel and all the things he already feels, just thinking about it. They graduated from the couch to his mattress and laid there, fully clothed, talking about it. He didn't even touch her.

"He didn't touch you?" I ask. I don't understand. Boys want to touch you. They want to stuff their hands up your shirt or down your pants. They want you to touch them. Boys say things like, "See how hard you make me?" And "Can't you feel how much I want you?"

"Didn't he want to?" I ask.

"He wanted it to be special," she said. So they made a date. A date to make love.

"Make love?" I say, but she just slants her eyes at me and maybe, I think, maybe I don't know anything.

We've moved inside. She's lying on the bed and I'm trying on her dresses in front of the full-length mirror. I like staring into my own eyes and wondering what I'm thinking. Sometimes my eyes tell me nothing, like I'm impenetrable.

"His apartment smelled like incense and the lights were really low." Toy's rushing now because she thinks she's lost my attention. We've already eaten the pizza and smoked some pot. Seth told her it was important that everything be done right.

I think about Todd's hand on my mouth. I'm tired of my own knocking thoughts about boys. Seth took off

Toy's dress and made her lie in front of him in her bra and underwear. He stroked her body with the tips of his fingers, then took off her underwear, parted her legs and licked her.

"He ate you out?"

"It wasn't like that," she says, and I think again, maybe I just don't know.

"He made me," she says, "ready."

Seth made her ready and then stood over her taking off his own clothes. He played her favorite music and made her breathe with him when he put himself inside her. I've never heard of a special kind of breathing, but Toy seems very certain. She says that he had a vase of flowers on each side of the bed and during, she rolled her head back and forth, looking from one to another. And she says that it hurt, but I say that's an old wives' tale because it hadn't hurt me at all. But she says it did.

"It hurt a lot," she says.

# my story

I tell Toy about Joey. I tell her about the ways we fit together. I was alone and then I found Joey, I say. "It was
love," I say.

Toy says, "Seth too. Love."

Then I tell her about Todd. The story I've been telling myself. "He wanted to kiss me," I say. "We had sex,
but it was a secret."

And Toy tells me about Seth, about how he kisses her
so lightly it's more like the thought of a kiss than a kiss
and I'm not even sure I know what that means.

Todd never kissed me and now I'm stuck on that. Like
a catch in the throat I can't get past. I can feel the sheets
and the pillow under my head and the air hitting my
thighs when he pulled down the blanket. Toy is going
on about Seth. How he kisses the inside of her wrists.
I'm dizzy from standing in two places at once, the night
at Delmi's party and here, now, in Toy's bedroom. I sit
down and Toy walks over and lifts my chin with her
hand. I want to tell her everything. A different story.

"Toy," I say and then I stop.

She's looking at me as if tuning in a channel, clearing the static. I rest my chin in her hand and look up. I think about her and Seth. How he must look at her. How well he must know her.

I don't tell Toy any other story. Instead I ask about Seth. It's exhausting, this not telling. I close my eyes. I can see the guest room in Delmi's parents' house. I'm nauseous and the bed is spinning. I have to concentrate on breathing. I open my eyes. I'm looking at Toy and thinking about Todd. I wonder if he ever thinks about me.

# tell-me-again times

I have to get out of the suburbs. I hold the idea so close, so tight, I could crush it.

I'm in my own bed. I have bad dreams. I kick free of the sweaty sheets and look at the pictures of girls I've ripped from magazines and pinned to my walls. One, faint, is of a girl in the forest, her head resting against another who sits just out of frame. I turn away, close my eyes, but the dream returns. I wake myself up and look back. My mom, just a kid in a faded photograph, meets my gaze.

It's the thin gray of morning and I strain to hear another person. I listen as though I could hear the family next door beginning to move around, as though I could hear my mom, wherever she is, waking.

I'm leaving, I think, and I feel better. I watch the light grow lighter.

"OK, then," I say aloud. "I'm leaving." I bury my head under the pillow and close my eyes. I shove my hands under my hip bones and tell myself the story, our story, my mom's and mine. I tell it again. I lie still and then I sleep.

# the camp counselor

Soon the bare walls are covered with pictures torn from magazines.

In one, two girls stand outside a medieval building in Paris and they're smoking. Their arms are hooked together in a "we're French and good friends" kind of way. Their long bangs almost cover their eyes and one wears a gauzy green skirt and a scarf over her hair. The other has thick, oddly shaped bangle bracelets around her skinny wrists. They're laughing. They're leaning together against the gray building.

I'm the girl in the green skirt. I'm French and my best friend is French and we smoke and laugh at the boys. We drink coffee in the cafes. Our mothers are fashionable and our fathers kiss us on both cheeks when they leave in the morning. The girl on the right looks slantwise at the other, but the girl in the green skirt stares straight out from under her bangs, right at the camera.

Toy is not French, but she's angular and beautiful. We're in the downstairs bathroom and smoking pot out of a homemade bong that leaks. It leaks all over my jeans, so I take them off and sit on the edge of the tub in my favorite underwear and my favorite striped T-shirt and watch Toy line her eyes with black pencil. She wears a black vintage dress because she loves Audrey Hepburn. I love Audrey Hepburn too and I've started to wear ankle-length pants and striped shirts, like in *Funny Face,* but neither of us resemble Audrey Hepburn in any real way. We're sixteen and Toy, I'm noticing, is cracked and uneven looking, with sly eyes and bony elbows and a strange little scar where her neck meets her collarbone. She had, I know, much worse stepfathers than mine.

This dress is cotton, with a deep V in the back and a high square neckline. We found it together at the dollar bins at Goodwill and after we washed it in her sink and hung it in the shower to dry, we both tried it on. So we both own it, but mostly Toy wears it. Sometimes we think that the perfect dress will change everything. Sometimes I'm jealous of the way it looks on Toy, who has long legs that stick out from under the dress like the legs of an elegantly carved table, even though hers are white and won't tan no matter how long she sits in her mother's backyard.

I watch Toy who's adding eye shadow on top of the pencil and heating up my curling iron so she can make little forties waves in the hair around her face. I'm watching, but I'm also holding my head aslant, chin down, looking up through my eyelashes and sneaking peeks at how I look in the mirror. I tuck my hair behind my ears and imagine myself with Toy's boyfriend, Seth. I want him to think I'm beautiful, like how he sees Toy. I want him to want something with me. Something real. He'll take my face in his hands or my hands in his hands and he'll stand close and say my name.

"Anna," he'll say.

All of this I imagine while staring into my own eyes in the bathroom mirror. Toy is talking and this is why I love her. She can go on about herself ceaselessly and like the scratching of a branch against the window at night, the steady insistence of it is comforting. She has stories without beginnings, stories that trail off, stories that crisscross and contradict and dead end.

Toy is the star of her stories. Events orbit her like a constellation.

In this story she's wearing the same dress that she's wearing now. She's waiting for the bus to come to my house when her camp counselor from the third grade drives by. It's late and the air is cool. She's without a sweater and watching the tiny bumps on her arm appear and disappear and reappear, so she doesn't notice when the camp counselor pulls alongside her.

He rolls the window down, tips his head to one side and says, "I recognize you. You're Toy."

And Toy says, "I recognize you, but I don't know your name. I remember that year at camp. I wore my favorite dress every day. It was red-and-white checkered with a white placket in the front and yellow buttons.

You said I should change if I wanted to play soccer with the other girls."

Toy looks at him as he idles by the bus stop in his faded blue car. Then she looks away, high into the pine trees that shield them from the sky and then she looks back.

She decides he's cute and she's calculating in that way so she drops her voice a bit, like a whisper that only he's meant to hear and she says, "I didn't want to play soccer with the other girls."

The camp counselor has vivid green eyes, dark brown curls, and the beginning of a beard in that way we both agree is sexy. He's wearing a Bauhaus T-shirt with blue jeans and Converse sneakers and his car's dirty, but in a college student kind of way with books and magazines and papers. Best of all, the camp counselor has a guitar case in the back, and in that way she has, Toy suggests that they go park by the lake and play his guitar.

Now is Toy's favorite part of the story. "It's the dress," she reprises. At an isolated bus stop, cast in miniature against a background of dark green pines, in a black dress, squinting at oncoming traffic, Toy is a skinny, third-grade girl all grown up. The camp counselor takes her to the lake and teaches her chords on the guitar. Everything glitters in the strong sunlight and when she closes her eyes and lies back against the grass, she feels his hand brushing the side of her cheek. And when she opens her eyes, he's looking down at her with a kind of wonder. He kisses her in a way that's tender and full of promise.

Toy squints at me in the mirror. I've dropped my shoulders, straightened my back and thrust my chest forward. I can feel the camp counselor's hand on the side of my cheek. My eyes are dropping closed and I can feel his breath next to my mouth. I put my hand out on the countertop.

In the mirror Toy is working on her lipstick. With the chords the camp counselor taught her, she says, she can play three new songs on the guitar.

# mom's boyfriends

It's nice you have a friend," my mom says. She comes home like a tourist. She changes her clothes and leaves. She doesn't ask where I was or where I'm going or who I'm with. She wants me to rinse the dishes before they go in the dishwasher. She wants me to take off my shoes before I come in the house. Sometimes she brings a man home and he waits in the kitchen while she changes her clothes. He's an Anthony or a Glenn.

I'm polite. I stand with my hands by my side.

"Nice to meet you," I say. We're in the kitchen where Joey liked to take off my shirt and kiss my chest. I'm making a bowl of cereal and Anthony is reaching out to shake my hand.

"Nice to meet you," I say again.

# get out of the suburbs
# as fast as you can

oy and I wear each other's clothes. I wear hers and roll up the sleeves. She wears mine and they look like doll's clothes on her. We buy dresses and share them. We shop at every thrift store in Portland. We take the bus to the east side, to the Salvation Army on Hawthorne or the Goodwill on Division. We're looking for the perfect dress, the one that will transform us.

And the city. The city! Only a bus ride away and full of possibilities. We get dressed up and do our makeup. We go downtown and stand around.

I belong here, I tell Toy. I'm hungry for every city block. Every brick building. Every crowded intersection. Electric. I feel brand new. My hair is shaggy and getting longer and I wear the wingtips with dresses from the forties and old-man cardigans. A broken leather belt knotted around my waist. Toy wears tunics over skinny jeans with high heels and thick socks.

"The city will transform us," I explain. "We'll never be alone."

But Toy's not alone. She has Seth. "And the camp counselor," she adds.

"He could come with us," I say. Sometimes about one and sometimes about the other.

"They're busy," Toy says. And I know what she means. She means they're only interested in her.

Sometimes, after I've gone home, one of them will pick up Toy and they'll go out. "Seth took me to his apartment," Toy will say the next morning, or she'll say something about the camp counselor, the way he holds her and how it makes her feel like it's only the two of them in the whole world.

I don't know what to say. Sometimes I forget about the city. Sometimes I want what Toy has. My life will never compare to Toy's. I feel sick with a fever of want.

# the boys skate around us

In the afternoons we go to the skatepark under the Burnside Bridge. We lean against the concrete barrier and watch the boys start and skate and stop again. They call out to each other and laugh. We meet a girl named Angel who carries vodka and orange juice in a jar. The three of us smoke pot and tell stories. Toy talks about Seth. Angel tells us about leaving home. About running away and ending up here. I watch how Angel tucks her hair behind her ear when she smokes. The boys skate around us and we pretend to shine them on.

# the empty house

I've had the dream again and I'm alone in my room. It's midday. I call Toy, but the phone just rings and rings. She's with Seth, I think, or the camp counselor, and I try to go back to sleep.

I'm in the kitchen eating cereal when my mom comes home.

"Is that all you ever eat?" She stands in the doorway wearing a white linen jacket, her purse in one hand. She doesn't sit down. She walks back into the kitchen and looks in the refrigerator.

"You should go grocery shopping," she says. And then she looks in her purse and pulls out two twenties. She's wearing high-heeled burgundy shoes with straps around the ankle and there's a streak of orangey makeup on her collar. I wonder if she's getting old and if this is what it's going to be like. Bits of her coming off on her clothes.

"Sure," I say, but she doesn't seem to hear me. She's looking through some papers, some mail on the shelf below the phone.

"You hate being here," I say. It's not a question. "You wanted this house so bad and now you're never here." Louder now. This lying house. I hate this house.

She looks up and then she looks confused. Then she looks at me in a way that makes me think she really does understand. This isn't what she wanted either. This empty house. But what does she want? Her face stretches tight over her cheekbones. Does she remember the tell-me-again times?

Up close her eyes are watery and bits of mascara litter her cheek. I can see how much makeup is on the collar of her jacket.

"I could stay home, Anna, if you want," she says, but she's looking back at the papers in her hand and hasn't put her purse down.

I'm done with my cereal. I take the bowl to the sink, rinse it, and put it in the dishwasher. "That's alright." I look past her into the still cul-de-sac. The sky's clear and cloudless. "I'm going downtown anyway."

# josh

Downtown the sun is back behind the bridge and there are only a few boys left, skating back and forth on the concrete ramp, dreamy and stoned. I meet a boy named Josh and he and Angel and I sit close together, our shoulders touching. We cup the end of the pipe for each other, sheltering the flame from the wind. I'm trying to describe the dream. I've had it ever since I can remember and it's familiar, but when I try to describe it, it breaks apart. The wind picks up and I shiver. I'm ready to give up because I can't make it sound right.

I stare at the changing sky and try again.

"I'm far from the world and I see it like a brightly lit ball in the distance. The sky behind it is mostly gray. It starts in silence, but I can see the people. Everyone is in a hurry. They're racing around the globe. They each hold a thread, like a bit of string, and it unravels, covering the planet. The buzzing starts. The buzzing gets faster and louder. They're all racing to one spot on the earth. I'm outside of it and I can see everything. I can see every person in the world racing to a single spot on the earth. The buzzing is all I can hear. It gets so I can't take it. Then I wake up."

Angel's sitting on my left.

"You're a stoner," she says. But Josh puts his arm around me.

"I know that feeling," he says. "It's like everything is standing still, but underneath it's all frantic and rushed."

I'm surprised and look at Josh full in the face. The boys are skating lazy figure eights and the sky is streaky with bits of light and stars showing through. I lean against him as he lights a cigarette and I feel good. Really good.

We go to his small apartment in Northwest to have sex. He looks right at me in a way that I almost don't understand and I look away but then I look back. He holds my eyes with his and even when I turn, he touches my chin and leads me back. His irises contract and the black centers have ragged edges. There's a distorted reflection of myself there, my own tiny face.

"Anna, Anna," he repeats like it's one long chant. "Anna, Anna, Anna, Anna." I keep staring into his eyes like he wants me to and he sits up with me on top, like we're hugging, but he's inside of me. "You," he says like there might be some kind of confusion, "are so beautiful, Anna."

And then he hugs me. Really hugs me. Like he thinks

that there's only one of me and I'm special and I'm enough for him. Like he doesn't need anything else. Like he was alone and then I came along and this is dumb, really dumb, because it feels so good and I like him more every second and I'm rehearsing how to tell Toy and because even though his apartment is ugly and small and the walls are yellow when they're supposed to be white, the streetlight through the curtainless windows does something; it makes our bodies pink and radiant and it fills the room with a kind of grace and this is the stupid part, I cry. Right there with him inside me. I cry really hard so the snot runs out of my nose and I have to wipe it on my arm.

This, I think, and I flash on Desmond Dreyfus and I flash on Joey and I flash on Todd, but this boy, Josh, is so solid I can feel the weight of him in my hands. I had no mother, I had no father, I start, as though it's my own story. I was all alone. And then I found you, I say, and then I say his name. Josh.

"I found you, Josh, and everything changed."

We have sex all that night and all morning. Fast and slow and fast again. My thighs sting and I have little bruises from where his fingers hold me. It isn't just the sex, I tell Toy in my head, it's his hands. His fingers. The way he needs me, because he's alone too. I can see it in his movements, his deliberate touch. And it's the me I see reflected, the thin grainy image of me, how it reflects in his serious eyes.

It rains, a summer rain that starts in the forgotten hours of morning and gets heavier and grayer and more punishing. There's no food at Josh's house and we've used all of his condoms and we're raw and sore and happy in a way that I imagine Toy means when she talks about sex with the camp counselor. I'm naked and he's watching me walk around his small rooms, touch his few things.

We get dressed and walk to Little Birds cafe in the slanting rain. It's Portland rain and the city folds under the weight of it, young trees bending in the wind. Josh takes my hand in his.

He orders for us at the counter and I take a seat, my fingers worrying an old gouge. The girl behind the counter nods at us and smiles at me. She has dreadlocks and I think, I always think this when I see girls with dreadlocks, that she knows something about herself that I don't know about myself. Our breakfast comes but Josh and I are looking at each other. The food grows cold in front of us. When the rain slows and the wind stops we go outside again and start walking south up the alphabet streets. Quimby, Pettygrove, Overton, Northrup, Marshall. Josh says the names under his breath and I watch the film of moving concrete under my sneakers, taking long steps to keep up with his. I had no father and I had no mother, I tell him again, and I describe the empty house. The silent carpet-covered halls and the aborted cul-de-sac. We walk down to the park blocks, in and out of shallow puddles, past the sculpture of Theodore Roosevelt and the one of Lincoln, then the abstract bronze shapes outside the art museum.

Josh is a story I tell myself. He's my Seth, my camp counselor. A story that's true. I'm telling myself the story of Josh and I look at his profile against the clouded sky.

"I was alone," I say aloud. "And then I found you." And when I say this he stops. We're standing in a puddle of leaves and rainwater and my feet are wet. It's cold, but I'm sweating and our breath is steaming. Everything is dripping. My chest moves up and down and I wait. Josh takes my chin and points my face up at the mottled gray sky. He looks serious, like he's going to kiss me, but he doesn't.

# toy

I tell Toy everything about Josh. He's the most romantic boy I've ever known, I tell her.

"Does he give you things?" she asks. "Presents?" She looks off into the distance. "Seth gave me a ring," she says and she gestures. I look at her hand, but she's not wearing it. "I'm not wearing it," she says.

"No," I say. "But he said he loves me," I tell her. "He whispered it," I say. I'd been waiting to tell her that. He'd whispered it against my back. His arms around me, his chin tucked between my shoulder blades.

"Oh," Toy says. And she looks at me hard, like she thinks I'm lying.

"He did," I say again. "And I love," I say, "the way he whispers things in my ear when we're having sex. Things that don't even make sense."

"Yeah," she says and she sounds wistful. "Seth does that."

# mom

My mom doesn't come home on Wednesday. Or on Thursday. So I practice telling her.

"I'm moving in with Josh," I'll say. Or I'll say, "Josh and I are in love."

Or maybe, "I have to get out of here."

"Who's Josh?" I imagine her saying. In my head she's angry and her manicured hands scatter the air by her face. She doesn't listen. She calls me ungrateful and ridiculous. She calls me juvenile. She breaks down and wet-eyed she leans in so her face is even with mine. She touches my cheek. "My baby," she says.

Other times I imagine that she's happy for me. She remembers the tell-me-again times and the apartment we shared. She takes my hand in hers and sits down on the bed, looking at our two hands in her lap. She asks about Josh. She asks about his apartment. She offers to buy us new sheets and a set of dishes. She talks about thread count, she talks about duvet covers. She looks at my face and I see myself in hers.

On Friday afternoon, she comes home to pack for the

weekend and when she rounds the corner with her dry cleaning, I'm waiting.

"Will you be alright?" she asks. She'll be home Monday, she says.

I follow her into the master bedroom. She pulls her suitcase out from under the bed and lays it open. She takes off her work clothes and stands in her slip.

"I'll be back on Monday," she says again. "Will you be alright?" She always asks that before she leaves. What if I said no? What if I said it's not alright?

She's wearing nylons under the slip and I can smell that warm smell she gets at the end of the day.

Maybe I'll tell her how much I hate this house. Maybe I'll describe the buzzing that follows me from room to room. How nothing drowns out the sound. Not the TV or the stereo or turning on every light in the house.

"I'm moving out," I say. "I'm moving in with Josh." But she doesn't hear me. She pulls a red-and-yellow dress from the closet and asks me to get her jewelry box so she can find her coral necklace. I stay still. I'm standing next to the bed and I say it again. I say it again and again and again. Josh gives me what I need, I say.

"I'm moving out."

Her mascara is smudged and I can see the reflection of the flat spot in the back of her hair in the mirror on the wall. She lays the red-and-yellow dress across the suitcase and moves to get her jewelry box. She's looking for the necklace that one of the stepfathers gave her. I lean back against the bed and look down at my boots. She hates it when I wear boots in the house.

She goes on packing and the suitcase fills with summer clothes.

"Mom?" I say. But she goes on. A pair of sandals, a light sweater, a silk scarf, some yellow pants. She takes a dress from the dry cleaner's bag and puts it on, hangs the other one in her closet. She zips up the suitcase and looks at me. Then she looks at her watch.

"You're going to do what you're going to do," she says.

She calls that weekend from the resort. She's thought about it, she says, and I can't go.

"I don't want to be the only one," she says, "alone in that big house." And then she says, "You don't appreciate what you have." Then she says that I don't love her. That Josh doesn't love me.

And how will I live? She won't give me any money.

I tell her that I love her and Josh loves me and that this is the best thing for everyone. I tell her that I'll get a job. That I'll work.

"I'm sixteen," I say. "I'm not a child."

I want to tell her about Josh and me. How it is between us. How he's my family now. How we'll live together and paint the walls of his apartment and how I'll hang pale blue curtains and cover the bed with my big down comforter. I'll take care of Josh and he'll take care of me, I want to say. Then I want to tell her my story. I had no mother, I had no father. Then Josh came along and everything changed.

"Everything's changed," I tell her. She doesn't ask about school, but I tell her anyway. I have a plan for that. "Kids leave all the time," I say. "I'll get a GED. That's what Josh did," I say. "And Angel." And when I say that she makes a noise.

"You'll be a dropout," she says. And then she hangs up.

A few minutes later she calls back. "Fine," she says. "Do what you want."

# the city

**G**et out of the suburbs as fast as you can, I tell
Toy.

I'm electric.

Does she see it? I want her to want what I have. I'm
going to live in the city. The city! I look at her side-
ways.

I pack. I look at every thing I own and imagine it in
Josh's apartment. I make piles. I pace around my room. In
this echoing house, I think, there's nothing I'll miss. And
my mom's gone again. Gone on the days I pack, missing
on the day I move.

But Toy's here, sitting on the side of my mattress,
burning matches, scraping my bowl and smoking a bit
of resin, not saying much. I'm leaving her, that's what
she thinks.

I sit down next to her with a shoe box. Even sitting,
she's so much taller than I am, angular and awkward.
She wears long blue gloves, up to her elbow, but takes
them off to scrape the pipe. I sit close, our thighs touch-

ing. She's intent on the pipe. I take the gloves in my hands and stroke the thin shiny fabric.

"Josh got me a fake ID," I say. But she's silent. In the shoe box are pictures of us from last year, taken with a Polaroid camera the stepfather left behind. In one, we're laughing on the back porch of an empty house in my neighborhood. We were drunk and dressed in taffeta party dresses from the fifties. Mine's green and I wear it with black Converse; hers is pink and she wears brown cowboy boots. We'd ratted our hair with a fine-tooth comb. Behind us the sun was setting, shifting and changing. Toy held my hand and toasted. To best friends, she'd said.

"Who needs boys?" I'd asked.

In another picture from the same night, she hangs over the railing like on a jungle gym, her face just visible between the bars. Her feet, in the battered cowboy boots, kick up, causing the taffeta to blossom around her legs. Even upside down she's arresting, with narrow eyes and a knowing mouth. She looks beyond the camera, beyond me, and if I turn the picture upside down, like I do now, it's like she's falling out of the sky. Just falling, right out of the sky.

She ignores the pictures and looks around the room, my bedroom that used to be the family room. "I'll miss it here," she says.

I look around at what used to be the stepbrother's room. And I think about the house like an architectural drawing, bisected so I can look into every empty room, all at once.

"I won't," I say and put the pictures back in the cardboard box.

# josh

Josh borrows a car to move me. It's the first time he's been to my house. He wanders from room to room with me trailing behind, our boots leave diminishing muddy footprints from the damp street outside.

With the pads of his fingers, he brushes the backs of the furniture, the glass vases, the framed pictures and I see, using his eyes, how everything is new and clean. How the glass objects, the bowls and balls, are free of dust. He sure didn't grow up in a house like this, he says. Am I sure I want to leave?

He stops in the upstairs bedroom, my old bedroom, the one from when I was a little girl. Nothing has changed. It's as though I still live there and I'm going to return home any minute and start playing with dolls.

Neat rows of stuffed animals are arranged along the wall. Music boxes queue up, on a high shelf, out of a child's reach. Josh walks over and stands in front of them. He's giant against the child-sized bureau. He fondles each music box in turn, holding them in his beautiful hands, turning them upside down to peer into their clockwork hearts. He turns a worn key in one and we listen.

My old bed is covered in a yellow comforter with a violet pattern. I sit down on it and Josh sits next to me. He puts his hand under my shirt and under my bra and holds my breast in the small of his hand. We sit like this, listening to the music box until it winds down.

# it's always romantic in the beginning

I drop out of school. It's easy. I get a paper and sign it. I leave it on the kitchen table for my mom to sign. The school signs it. School's over. I pass Nancy Baxter on my way out of the front doors and she's hurrying to class but turns to look at me. Bye, Nancy Baxter, I think. And then I think: she doesn't mean anything to me anymore.

I call Toy. "I did it," I say. "Don't you want to do it too?"


I get a job in a cafe. I make espressos, cappuccinos, lattes. I make nine dollars an hour and tips in a jar. Nobody asks about my parents. Nobody says, why aren't you in school? Nobody says, where's your mother? Nobody ever says, where's your father? But I rehearse the conversation. "There are no fathers in this story," I'll say. I think it's a very good line.

But I look for him. My useless father. I look for him at the cafe. On the street.

* * *

I move my boxes into Josh's apartment. I put my comforter on his bed. I lie spread out on top of the bed, fully
dressed breathing in and out through my mouth with
my eyes wide open staring at the ceiling. Now I'm here
and I live here and even though my boxes of things don't
seem to make much of a difference and the apartment is
still artless and bare, I'm here. And when I breathe here
it's different. I stretch my arms wide open and take it
all in.

"Hug me," I say.

"Kiss me," I say. And Josh tells me about all the things
he's done and I sit across from him in one of his two big
chairs and I listen. We put on our coats and walk around
the neighborhood. We walk out to the river, past the
empty warehouses and the old rubber factory. We walk
up the hill to where the rich houses are and steal a stone
statue of a cherub out of someone's garden. We put it
next to our bed. I love you, I tell Josh. I've always loved
you, he tells me.

I call Toy and tell her how romantic it is. "I say I love
you and he says I always loved you." She doesn't say anything. "Isn't that romantic?" I ask.

She doesn't answer. She's distracted. I can hear her at
the stove and know that she's scrambling eggs for her
mom. She gets scared, I know, because her mom doesn't
eat.

"I want you to meet him," I say.

"There's a lot going on for me," Toy says.

"Your mom."

"No." She sounds sharp and I can hear her mom in the background. "It's Seth," she says. "He has something special planned." Even with my new apartment, Toy's life sounds more romantic than mine. I miss her. I turn everything I see into a story to tell her.

"I miss you," I say. I've lived with Josh for two weeks and she hasn't visited at all.

I call Angel then, and walk up to her apartment. It's small and she's painted the walls red—she'll never get her deposit back, she says—and admire the row of antique dresses that separates the sitting area from her bed. I run my hands along the paper-thin silk, too delicate to wear.

I'm wearing my uniform, a long men's cardigan with my favorite faded T-shirt and gray jeans with Converse sneakers. I can see a sliver of my reflection in Angel's mirror and I look like the girl I imagined I'd be. I want to call Toy again and tell her.

Angel asks me about Josh and I tell her that he likes it when I fall asleep with my head on his chest. I tell her how he keeps me wrapped up in his arms all night. How romantic it is, how he's loved me forever.

She knows how it is with boys. "It's always romantic in the beginning," she says.

# winter

Josh wakes me up in the middle of the night to have sex. Sometimes he kneels over me and holds my wrists above my head. Sometimes he pulls me on top and I rock back and forth until he comes. I get up early to go to work. The apartment is so cold that I have to kneel in front of the space heater to get dressed. It's winter. It isn't the apartment I'd imagined it would be.

My fake ID belongs to a girl named Elizabeth Ray Clark. She lives in Seattle and kind of looks like me. In her picture she has gray-blue eyes that look like mine. She squints through her eyelashes. I pretend to be her. I go by Liz, Lizzie. Lizbeth if you know me really well. My family calls me Beth. I live in my own apartment in Seattle with exposed brick walls and big windows, high ceilings and hardwood floors. I have sheer yellow curtains that bathe the room in warm colored light. I have a best friend who comes over and hangs out with me and a bicycle that I ride around the city. It has a basket. And I have a boyfriend. He's funny and kind and he likes to write little notes and leave them around the apartment.

Josh doesn't write little notes. He was out of work when we met but now he has a job painting houses. He's tired all the time. He's nineteen. He's pale and skinny and he doesn't seem to want anything more than this.

"I work too," I say, but he says it's not the same. He says I'm a spoiled rich kid who doesn't know what it's like in the real world. He says I'm just playing at it. I'm slumming.

"I don't want to spend my one day off painting," he says when I ask if we can paint the apartment.

The apartment is desolate. It swallows up all the pretty things I brought. I miss Toy. We're in the tunnel of winter now and it's always cold. Too cold to sit in the big chairs and talk. Instead we drink. We meet at the bar after we get off work. Josh teaches me to say what's on tap, and how to choose the best of the cheap beers, and how, when I want to get drunk faster, to order tequila and drink it with lime and salt. He rests both elbows on the bar, head hanging between, like something collapsed.

Josh's stories loop so that now, after only a few months, I've heard them all. It gets dark early. We avoid the apartment and stay at the bar. We eat cheap takeout. Or we make macaroni and cheese from a box. I hang the dresses that Toy and I bought at thrift stores—the blue velvet one, the black one with the rhinestones, the solid ones and the ones with stripes. They make the prettiest spot in the apartment. I rest my eyes there. Toy never comes to visit.

I call from the pay phone after work. Her mom answers. She never answers. She slurs a word that sounds like hello and then she laughs. She makes another noise, like a protest, and then Toy comes on the line. It sounds like her mom is crying in the background.

"Toy? Are you OK?" I say.

"Anna," she says, her voice changing, and then she's quiet. When she talks again, she sounds dreamy. "I met a boy," she says. "He has the most beautiful green eyes you ever saw."

"You said you'd come visit," I say, but she goes on about the boy. He's seventeen, a senior in her high school.

"You could both come," I say. But he's busy, planning a trip. He's going to hostel through Europe and he's invited her along, she says. They'll start in Berlin and then travel north to Sweden, he has family in Stockholm, and then back south to lie on the beach. Italy, Spain, Portugal. They'll leave next summer when school is out. She has no idea what she'll wear.

"That's a long time from now," I say, but she ignores me. He's the most romantic boy I could ever imagine, she says. And so thoughtful. In the middle of the night he comes over and sneaks into her bedroom. They kiss for hours, she says. He brings her things, jewelry, and lingerie. He buys her dresses.

"You should see the dress he bought me," she says.

"Come show me," I say, but she can't. "Then I'll come over to you," I say.

"No," she says. She's busy.

I'm wearing heavy boots and a pale blue dress with a thick gray sweater and my heavy coat. I leave the pay phone. I storm through the streets, up to Fourteenth, across to Pettygrove, down to Third and Kearney. I'm not like Josh. I do want more. I pace up and down the alphabet. Even when it's not raining, the trees drip water. I end up at Paranoia Park where I smoke dope under the bushes with some people I know there and we look out at the businessmen crossing stiffly through the park. We smoke each other's pot. It's Thursday and I'm supposed to have dinner with my mom. I'm late.

"Have you been smoking pot?" she asks, narrowing her eyes and looking into mine. I tell her that I like her coat, that it looks pretty on her. The hostess shows us to a table. I'm wearing my military coat and I know that she doesn't think much of it, but I like the way it buttons tightly around my chest and it's long, longer than my dress and it flaps between my legs when I walk.

We sit down and she orders a glass of wine. "Have you had enough?" she asks, before I know what she's talking about. Then, "Are you ready to come home?"

I look at the menu. "No," I say.

# the apartment

J osh isn't home when I get back and the apartment's cold. So cold I can see my breath. I feel around in the dark because we haven't replaced the overhead bulb and I make my way over to the old ceramic lamp sitting on the floor. It doesn't light the room, just a bright circle at its base, so I sit next to it and empty out my tips like I do every night: count the change, save the quarters for laundry, face the bills the same way. I have forty-six dollars.

I put sixteen dollars in the pocket of my coat and tuck thirty in an envelope that I keep in the bottom drawer of Josh's dresser. I put the envelope away and close the drawer. Then I open it again. I pull out the envelope and count the money. Four hundred and twenty-eight dollars in bills, all facing the same way. I put it back in the envelope, back in the drawer, and go out to look for him.

There's a fresh wind outside and I don't have a scarf. I hold the collar of my coat closed around my neck and look both ways when I leave the apartment. Under a coffee-colored sky, the block is empty. A streetlamp flickers and goes out and I think of Toy. Josh isn't at the bar so I walk on, but he isn't at the coffee shop either.

When I get back he's at the apartment, sitting on the floor by the mustard-colored lamp, looking blank. He looks like that more often lately, like an object out of place, or maybe I'm the object out of place, or maybe he's always looked like that and I'm just now noticing.

The apartment unfolds in the dim light. The unmade bed is peaked and stormy, the sheets I brought are now as dingy as everything else.

I know he's tired. I know he's worked all day. His face is freckled with paint and he has clumps of it in his hair. I sit next to him so I don't block the space heater and I begin to untie his boots. The laces are long and broken and mended in little knots. I untie each one in turn and loosen the tongue. His socks are bunched painfully beneath. I open his boots and pull them off, smooth his socks over thin ankles and hold the feet together, whispering, "Poor feet, poor feet," into the arch of each one.

He stiffens. He's self-conscious about his feet. But I hold them tight under the arch until he relaxes, pulls his knees to his chest and closes his eyes. I feel that I can take care of him. I run my hands over his calves and knead the muscles. Then, slowly so he doesn't flinch, I take off his socks and run my palms over the soles of his feet.

I want to take care of him. I pick the little balls of cotton from between his toes and smooth the skin. I take off my own boots and socks and place our feet together by the heater, unbutton my coat and push it to the floor. Josh reaches over and pulls off my shirt, my stretchy bra, and pulls me, half undressed, on top of him. In the light from the mustard-colored lamp, my skin is pale and my breasts are pointy. The nipples are too large and I'm embarrassed by them. He's holding me at arm's length, looking at my chest. My belly pudges out and my arms are childish, but he's kissing me and looking at me with eyes open or closed, and it doesn't matter.

The part of me in front of the space heater is burning. The other parts retreat in the cold air. His hands warm me, like hands petting a cat, but my skin chills as soon as his touch leaves. He gets to his knees, picks me up like a child, and carries me to our wintry, indifferent bed. He covers me with the dirty sheet and the big down comforter and then he sits there, just watching me.

"I thought we were going to make love," I say.

# all of me

I stand in our bathroom trying to find my reflection. The dream is a low hum at the edge of everything. The room is dim and the mirror is stained with rust, so even standing as far back as I can, on my toes, I can only see a thin reflection. She doesn't even look like me.

I had no mother, I tell the wavering image. I had no father.

But nothing's changed, the reflection replies.

Suddenly I want to go back to the suburbs and the pull is sharp and quick. Unexpected. I have to get out of the apartment. I call my mom but she isn't home and I'm not sure if I'm disappointed or relieved.

It's nearly midnight. There are four other girls on the bus, sprawled out in the back, headed home after a night in the city with their heavy makeup and black clothes. They're maybe fourteen and they have a kind of happy kid–ness that shines through the sullen facade. They giggle and then catch themselves and smirk.

They're girls, I think, so their future is certain and I think about Toy. She has all these boys. All these boys that think she's beautiful. That give her things, but what's the use? She's still afraid.

Afraid for her mom. Afraid she is her mom. What's the use?

I watch the girls' reflection in the dirty glass. We're circling a long on-ramp headed toward the freeway. I lean against the window and look out into the darkness.

In the suburbs, the streets are smaller and narrower than I remember. It's only been six months since I left, but already I'm out of place. Still, my key fits easily in my mom's lock and the door swings open. The house is hushed. I don't know where I belong. I push the dial on the thermostat, all the way up until I hear the rush of the furnace.

With Josh's eyes I notice the insistent cleanliness of everything. Nothing chipped or worn. I leave the lights off and drop my bag. In the hall off the entry I slide down a familiar wall until I'm sitting over a heating vent, the warm air rushes out and I pull my T-shirt over my knees to catch it, just like I did when I was little.

I'm tired. Not because it's late or because I worked today. Not because I made cappuccinos and lattes and caffe americanos. Not because I slept in a tight ball on one side of the bed since Josh started saying that I kick too much. Since he won't sleep tangled with me anymore. It's a new tired.

I make a bowl of cereal and turn on the TV. I sit on one of the big chairs in the living room and imagine my mom coming home. Finding me. I imagine what she'd say and maybe she'd just be happy to have me back. I'm not back, but being here feels like gravity. Weighty. Pulling at me. I turn off the TV and in the upstairs bathroom I start a bath and take off all my clothes. Heavy and tired.

In the water I watch my feet emerge, disconnected in the far end of the tub. This is me, I think, and I sit up suddenly, like a revelation. I hook my knees over the edge, stare at the curve of my stomach, my bent legs, my feet and I think, this is it. This is all of it. This is everything. And it's not like waiting. And it's not like imagining. And it's not like a story I tell myself. Maybe, I think, it's not boys. It's not Josh. Or Joey. It's not this empty house. Or Josh's cold apartment. I climb out of the tub and stand naked in front of my mom's fulllength mirror. All I can hear is the furnace. This is all of me, I think, and I stretch out my arms like a fivepointed star. I'm looking at my hair and how it's grown, how my eyes are just visible below my bangs. I'm looking at my hands and my elbows. I'm staring into my own eyes and whatever it is, whatever it is that I want so badly, that thing that Josh doesn't understand, that my mom doesn't see, maybe that's all I need. The furnace clicks off and I wrap myself in a large towel. I climb into my mom's bed and burrow under the clean sheets. I've left the milk out and in the morning it's warm.

# the next morning

I'm pregnant. I haven't taken the test but I know.

My mom's stories loop in my head. "All I wanted was a little girl," she said. "And then you came along and I had everything."

But I'm not everything. I'm not even enough to keep her home.

I call Toy and she comes over. Her mom brings her to my mom's house and when I go to the curb to meet them, her mom calls me over to the car window. I lean down.

"Are you finally moving home?" she asks. She's wearing a coat over her nightgown and a scarf over her hair. Her eyes are fragile and red-rimmed.

"No," I tell her. "I'm not," I say and I trail off and we both look at the house. But I try to be polite. I know that Toy's mom doesn't really see me. She's like my mom that way. My mom doesn't really see Toy either.

Toy's mom idles in the cul-de-sac in front of my mom's house.

"Come on," Toy says to me and I start to say more,

but her mom squints at me through the open window and I can tell she's not listening. I step back and she pulls away from the curb.

Toy takes me by the hand straight into the house, down the stairs to the room that used to be the family room. Just like we used to. Even though there isn't any furniture down there anymore and the walls are covered with primer because my mom's going to redecorate, turn it back into a family room.

We collapse against one wall and Toy loads the soapstone pipe, gives the bowl and the lighter to me and sucks in her breath.

"OK, tell me everything."

There's not much to tell. There were so many times when Josh just pulled out and came on my stomach.

"I want to feel you," he'd said.

"He did?" Toy says.

"They all say that," I say. Doesn't she know that? I tap the pot down with my finger and light the edge. "I already called the clinic," I tell her. "Four hundred bucks."

"You think he'll pay?"

"Half, I think," and I think he will.

Toy holds my hand. She's always at her best when I'm at my worst. We sit with our backs against the wall, my hand in hers, looking out the sliding glass door at the damp grass. The yard has begun to bloom with spring flowers. The room is cold because the vents are closed and I can see all the spots on the carpet where Toy and

I spilled candle wax staying up late and smoking pot and talking.

"Strange in here now," says Toy.

"Yeah," I say and I pack my bag and we wait for the bus to go back downtown.

# jane

Three days later I'm in the Women's Health Center talking to a woman named Jane. She's pregnant. The woman at the abortion clinic is pregnant and I save the irony to share with Toy. I tell Jane about my breasts, how they're swollen and sore. How I'm nauseous. She tells me a trick: if I eat saltines before I even lift my head from the pillow, I won't throw up. As soon as I leave the clinic I'll buy some saltines.

Jane has clean, freckled skin and warm pudgy hands. I think she would reach over and pat me on the arm if it looked like I needed that. She has large pregnant breasts and her thick cotton T-shirt pulls around her stomach. I can see the outline of her belly button. She wants to know how I got pregnant. How I feel about the pregnancy. If I've told the boy, if I've told my mom, if I've thought about keeping the baby.

"No," I say. Her eyes scan my face and when I tell her about Josh, she tips her head and gives me a sympathetic nod. I tell her about the cold apartment. My dim reflection in the bathroom mirror. She would spend hours talking to me, I think. We'd stay here until I ran out of things to say. I tell her things. I think about Todd and the night at Delmi's house and I almost tell her, but then I don't.

"Have you ever had an abortion?" I ask.

"I was a little older than you," she says. And she tells me how angry her parents were. How her mom cried. Now, she says, she's thirty-three. She's been married for three years.

"And soon," she says, with her hand on her stomach, "there will be three of us."

When I look at her, tracing the spots on her cheek where the freckles all run together, I think maybe she's the first happy woman I've ever met.

We talk about names for the baby.

"Anna's a pretty name," she says. She's having a girl.

The room has anatomically correct drawings of the female reproductive system on the wall and no windows. I take a plastic replica of a pelvis from the desk and turn it over and over in my hands.

"Do you usually use condoms?" she asks. "How many sexual partners have you had?"

Jane doesn't judge. "You're not supposed to judge," I say like it's a statement. And she's surprised that I live with Josh. She asks if I like it. If I miss school. But school's not what I miss.

"It's not like I thought it would be," I say, because it's not. And then she asks about my mom. She asks about my dad.

"I don't know about fathers," I say. I've been waiting to use that line. I've been waiting for someone to ask. She laughs and I feel really happy. I'd wanted to make her laugh. We're laughing and, thinking about her daughter, I say, "You should name her Joy."

And she says, "Don't you think that's a little obvious?" And she says, "Wouldn't it be better to have a name with a little mystery?" and then she laughs again. "Are you ready for a pelvic exam?" she says.

Josh is good about the four hundred dollars. He's going to borrow the money from his boss, he says, most of it. We meet at the bar and talk about it. He's going to pay most of it, he says and he says it again, "Most of it." And then again.

"It's my responsibility," he says.

He holds his beer with both hands and his long fingers circle the glass. His hair is long and littered with paint. He looks tired.

I didn't tell Jane my mom's story. I didn't tell her that I'd made it mine. I have no mother, I'd told Josh. I have no father. Then Josh came along and changed everything. Now I was pregnant, but even I knew this wasn't going to change anything.

Josh doesn't ask about my story. He asks if I'm OK.

"I'm OK," I say. And it's true. That feeling from the

night at my mom's hasn't gone away. That view of myself: arms and legs and eyes steady in the mirror, that hasn't left me. All of me, I think. I still have that.

"I'm OK," I say again.

He's going to borrow a car to take me to the clinic. He'll come in and stay while it's happening. The abortion, he says. "I'll take you there and I'll wait. I'll be there," he says, "while you're having the abortion." He spins around on his bar seat. He doesn't ask any of the questions that Jane asked. He doesn't ask how it happened. He doesn't ask if I want to keep it. He asks which day and when, how long will it take.

"Are you scared?" he asks. And he pulls me off balance against his chest. He puts his mouth against my ear and holds me, making noises, breathing, smashing my face against his shirt. He smells dusty like dried paint and I pull away. I pull myself back on the bar stool next to him. We spend the evening shooting pool and he makes a big deal out of the shots I make.

"Do you want to go home?" he says, leaning against me, and I do. I lean against his dusty smell and lace my fingers with him. I'm going to leave him, I know. My mom's story is not my story. I'm going to need a new story. I wrap my coat around me and let him lead me back to the apartment.

# the abortion

I'm ready. I have two days off work and then it's the weekend. I tell my mom over the phone.

"I knew this would happen," she says.

"Will you come?" I ask and she's quiet. And I think it's because I don't ask. I never ask.

"Anna," she says and there is everything there in my name.

It's decided. Josh will pick me up and Toy and my mom will meet us at the apartment, after. When I get to the clinic, Jane is sitting behind the counter.

"Can you go in there with me?" I ask her. There are other girls, other women, other uncomfortable boyfriends in the waiting room. There are parents, everyone judging everyone else.

"Sure, Anna," she says and she hands me some paperwork. She doesn't try to look past me to where Josh's already hunched down in a chair.

They call me in to give me some valium. They take my blood pressure. The nurse, who leans over me with two pills and a paper cup, smells like cucumber. She smiles and pats my arm and then holds my hand, reassuring me in a way that tells me I'm scared even though I hadn't known that I was. She reminds me of Jane and for a moment I think they might be sisters, even though I'm sure they're not.

The women here all have these warm smiles. The kind where someone looks right at you and sees you. I lean back against the pale green wall and close my eyes, but she tells me to go back to the waiting room, that it won't be long. She wants the valium to relax me and then, she says, when I come back, Jane will be there.

I go back out to the waiting room. I hold Josh's hand. I think: I'm holding his hand because he's scared and he needs me, and I'm right about that. My hand is on top of his. His skin is very pale and he looks at the ground between his feet.

They take me into a small room. The doctor comes in and introduces himself. He's wearing scrubs. He makes a joke. "I'm a good doctor," he says, "but my taste in fashion is questionable." He laughs and then Jane comes in.

She touches my cheek and says, "Anna," as though we're old friends who've just picked up a long-running conversation, "I've been thinking." And she moves in closer to whisper. "I want to name her Imogen."

I taste the name in my mouth. People are moving around the room, setting up. A nurse puts my feet in the stirrups and Jane takes my hand. There's a single lamp with four bulbs on the ceiling and the nurse leans in to tell me what to expect. She warns me before they give me a shot to numb my lower half and then she tells the doctor that I'm ready. I look around the room at the two nurses and the doctor in scrubs. I look at Jane. She's glowing in that way they say that pregnant women glow. She looks very calm and I feel, looking at her, something new. Something calm.

Imogen.

"I like it," I say.

# after the abortion

Cramping. Tugging. Pulling. I sleep afterward in a room with other girls. How am I feeling? Nurses float around me, bring paper cups of water, murmur, women sleeping and waking. No Jane. She'll be back later, someone says.

I sleep again. My mom is in my dreams. My stuffed animals lined up, the small ones in the front, and we're telling the story. Tell us again, they say. My mom wraps me in her arms. I'm a five-pointed star. We tell our story, but it's a different story.

Jane is there. "Can you sit up?" she asks and I can. I sit up and the room comes into focus. Jane's face is serious and she sits by the side of the bed and looks at me as though judging if I'm alright.

"I'm alright," I say.

"Are you ready to leave?" she asks, and I am.

\* \* \*

Josh is quiet as he helps me to the car. He holds my arm tight and makes sure I buckle my seat belt before he closes the passenger side door.

"I'm alright," I say when he gets behind the steering wheel, but he doesn't start the car. "Josh," I say and I take his chin in my hand until he meets my eyes. "I'm alright."

In front of the apartment building, Toy materializes. My sister. My other half. She dismisses Josh. He stands there, no longer useful, until she repeats, "Go back to work, Josh." She'll take care of me, she says. Josh transfers my arm to hers and steps back.

"It's OK," I say and I lean into Toy's embrace. And then Toy, in charge, opens the door of the apartment and moves me into the bed. My mom helps her, pulling back the covers and it's strange to see them together, my mom and Toy. How the abortion makes us a family.

The room is warm, too warm. Toy's lit candles and there's music coming from my little player. My mom then, suddenly, hugging me, enveloping me, loving me. Why now? I'm trying to make sense of it.

Toy brings me a hot chocolate in my favorite blue mug. They tuck some pillows behind me so I can sit up and drink. My mom looks out of place in the dim apartment, drinking in small sips from the other mug, the chipped yellow one. She's watching Toy. Toy plays music, Billie Holiday and Édith Piaf, and runs around moving candles and laying out chips like it's a party. She's talking, Toy is always talking. She's talking about "Gloomy Sunday."

"Yes," my mom says. "That's a very sad song." Her hand is in mine. She starts telling our story in a faraway voice. She had no father, no mother. She was all alone until I came along.

"And then you came along and everything changed," she says and her hand is still in mine and she's looking down at me and seeing all the ways I look like her and I know she believes it. She forgets about the other stories she tells herself. The one about the next husband and then the next. I'm so tired, so heavy, but I struggle to protest.

"That's not our story anymore," I say. But I'm asleep and I'm not sure I say it out loud.

# sleep

When I wake my mom is gone. Toy is stretched out next to me, asleep. I can make out Josh's figure in the big chair. It's black outside the window and the room is terribly hot. I hurt all over and I take one of the pain pills with a bit of cold cocoa. Then I sleep.

# josh

After the abortion, Angel moves to Seattle.

"Portland is so over," she says.

I'm standing in her apartment with the red walls. Her clothes are boxed up and her furniture is gone. It looks like any room now. We sit on the floor with the pipe and a lighter and a bottle of wine between us. I'm talking about Josh, but I'm thinking about abortion and it mixes together, my stories. The empty house, the curtainless windows in Josh's apartment, the girl I want to be.

Angel knows how it is. "This isn't about Josh," she says.

And I think about this: Toy and my mom together by the side of my bed listening to Billie Holiday and drinking cocoa.

I can't stand how everything stays the same. Toy disappears again. The apartment is empty. Josh goes to work and afterward he meets me at the bar. He tells the same stories to the same people and he touches my hand the same way when it's time to leave. Even the trees on the sidewalk are bare and the buzzing's back. Faint like a shadow, but there. Like all the people on earth are racing to a single point.

At the cafe I stare in people's faces and they catch me, watching. I'm looking for something. Someone. Some sign that I've changed. It's Thursday and I leave the cafe and walk up the park blocks and over to the university. Down to the river and past the fountain and over to the train station. I stare at the buildings looking for the one where I lived with my mom. And then I find it. Not the same one, but one that's squat and brick like ours was. It's short and solid with painted window frames and a FOR RENT sign in the window.

I know what I'm going to do.

I call Toy. I stand at the pay phone across the street from the apartment and memorize the manager's number, four-oh-one-eight-six-seven-nine. I wait for Toy to answer and I repeat it to myself, four-oh-one-eight-six-seven-nine.

Hello, I say, to the little building. I'm going to live here.

But Toy doesn't answer, so I call the manager and set up an appointment for the next day. Then I call Toy again.

"I'm moving out," I say and the words come out in a rush, but Toy isn't listening. She sounds distracted and distant and suddenly I have to picture myself without a best friend. I keep talking about the building and the street and the manager's creaky voice and I keep talking because I don't know what else to do.

Then I hear it. She lightens and I can hear her listening. I can picture her, ear pressed to the phone, sucking on her lip like she does, breathing softly, and I imagine that she's remembering me in the way I need to be remembered.

"OK," she says meaning she's going to come. I lean against the phone booth and breathe out, rubbing the toe of one damp boot against the other.

# my own apartment

The next day I make fifty-seven cappuccinos, thirty-nine lattes, twenty-two espressos and nineteen caffe americanos. Toy walks into the cafe and it's as though I don't know even her. It's as though she has some life that I'm not even a part of. And she does, I know. Boys who look at her with soft round eyes, who give her things, who want her. She looks new, like she doesn't need me. Like she never needed me. Wearing skinny jeans on her long legs and bunched-up olive-colored leg warmers over pointy boots. She has a narrow navy wool coat and a striped scarf and she looks like someone I only wish I knew.

I'm wearing a dress, but it's cotton and covered in a sweater and it doesn't fit quite right and I think that maybe she won't see me. I have to look away and I go back to cleaning the counter and I think, for a second I think: She's not even going to see me. She's going to walk right back out again. But she doesn't. She walks over when I'm taking off my apron and she doesn't hesitate. She hugs me like she always does. Like nothing's changed.

And then, in that way she has, she takes my arm and it's like, of course, everyone wants to be us.

We leave the cafe arm in arm. We go to Avalon to look at dresses. We go to Django's to look at music. We're killing time until it's time to look at the apartment. Finally I take her to Eleventh and Alder and stand her in front.

"This is it," I say. I want her to say something that means she knows how important it is.

She does, she takes my hand in hers. "Oh," she says and she breathes out through her mouth. "Your own apartment."

She understands! "My own apartment," I say and now I think things really will be different. "My own apartment," I say again. It will be filled with pictures of beautiful girls and dresses and jewelry and music and—

Then she looks around. I want her to want what I have. I want her to say, "I wish I could leave home too," but she doesn't.

"But why don't you just move back home?" she says.

Spring is already showing and I'm sweating inside my coat. I could, I know. I could just go home. Right now. And forget the cafe and the women who tap their nails against the counter while they wait for their cappuccinos. I could go home. Leave right now and never come back. I could just pack my bag and move back into my mom's house.

That empty, gaping house.

I look up at the little brick building. It's flat and it's ugly and the paint on the window frames is peeling and I think about this thing, this thing that makes me hurtle forward because I can't go back. The big house and the aborted cul-de-sac and the empty rooms and I know there has to be something better and I don't even care if this is it.

"No," I say and we ring the bell for the manager.

Then I'm standing in my own apartment. I can feel the weight of it on my skin. The manager's face is suspicious, sunken. Toy is talking in a funny grown-up voice about the strange view and the manager is looking at her and at me and saying that the apartment is too small for two people.

I walk from one end of the apartment to the other, my hand trailing along the bare walls. The apartment is small and I can see the front door from the tiny kitchen. The odd little bathroom has high ceilings and a claw-foot tub. My own apartment.

"It'll just be me," I say. In a drawer in Josh's apartment I have an envelope with $1,146 that I've saved. The manager's caved features drop into a smile.

# toy

**W**e're back in the park blocks, under the steady stare of Teddy Roosevelt on horseback. THEODORE ROOSEVELT ROUGH RIDER, the plaque says.

Toy reads it out loud. "Rough Rider," she says. We think it's hilarious. We sit shoulder to shoulder and the immobile president watches Toy load the soapstone pipe. I stare through the trees at the pale gray sky thinking about the apartment.

But Toy's met someone. Finn, a boy from another high school. A boy with green eyes. A boy who's punk and funny and wants to be a filmmaker. He wants Toy to star in his films.

She pauses, and I know what she's saying. No one has ever asked me to be in a film.

"What about the other one," I say. "The one . . ." I trail off. "Remember?" I'm thinking about the one—am I mistaken? The one who wanted to take her to Europe. And I realize that it is, actually, easier to talk about Toy than to talk about myself.

"Oh," she says. "He still loves me, but I don't know." She makes a pile of leaves with the toe of her boot. "I still call him sometimes."

"I've missed you," I say before I realize I've said it and I mean since the abortion. I don't ask her why she hasn't visited because I know. Finn and Seth and the camp counselor and the other one. All the other ones.

And I think, maybe it's OK that Toy doesn't want what I want. Like maybe she's the one who does some things, like be in Finn's movies, but I'm the one that does other things. Maybe I'm the one that had to move on, and maybe, someday, she'll follow. Maybe I'm the one who has to go first no matter what it takes.

Toy gives me the first hit which is a sign of affection or a kind of honor between us. I poke my hand out of the cuff of my coat and take the pipe. Toy's talking about Finn, but she says she likes this dress on me. It's one we bought together, a kind of plaid, green-and-black housedress from the sixties. I wear it with black tights and boots and a belt knotted around my waist.

We recline on the bench, our four feet in front of us and the pipe moving back and forth between us. I want to tell her about Josh. How it's changed. Or how it was never what I thought it was, and how Angel says it's not really about Josh.

And I want to ask her if it's like that for her. If Finn. Or maybe Seth and the camp counselor, if it's beginning to pale and diminish the way it did with Josh. The way, I think, it did for her mom. The way it did for my mom.

How my dad, her dad, after a time, were of no use at all.

I want to tell her about the $1,146. How I keep it in an envelope in one of the two drawers that are mine in Josh's dresser. How I like to count it. How I add to it and subtract from it and how I keep the number in my head like a secret sign. I want to tell her how I feel when I picture the envelope there, in its drawer. How it makes me feel better and strong, and how, when I'm at work, I picture it in the drawer under the black sweater and the gray T-shirt. How I can feel its thickening weight. How it will feel when I spend it on the new apartment. And I'm not sure why, but maybe if we talked about it, I would understand why this little collection of rooms makes me feel less alone. And I'd like to. Talk about it.

But Toy is asking about a dress. A blue velvet dress from the fifties that we bought together and sometimes I keep and sometimes she does. She's talking about some shoes she has, that would be perfect for the dress and how she wants to wear the dress in a film Finn is making. I should give her the dress, she says.

Sometimes I just let Toy talk. Sometimes I interrupt her. Just wedge something else in, something important, like the envelope. Mostly she doesn't even notice.

She has something to say about everything. About anything. But I don't do that now. I listen to her talk about the dress. I picture it hanging on a hook, unworn, in Josh's apartment.

"Sure," I say. And I say that I'll give it to her and maybe, I say, she can give me the green glass beads. The ones we found in a bag of junk jewelry at Salvation Army and then fought over who would keep them.

That reminds her. The beads remind her of Finn and the short film he made. A kind of fairy tale, she says, starring his little sister, Viv. The little sister, Toy says, is an angel.

"She's a doll," Toy says. "An angel."

I think about emptying my tip jar every day and counting the money. I think about the walk from the apartment to work and from work to the apartment. I think about Josh and my funny dim reflection in the bathroom mirror. I think about Jane and the women at the clinic and the way I picture Jane filling her home with the people she loves. Look what's happening to me, I want to say. Can't you see?

There's a vertiginous moment when Toy is all angles and the statue of Teddy Roosevelt is looking down. Jagged naked trees with small green buds loom over us. I hear a buzzing, like everyone racing but standing still and I wish I could climb inside her so she could love me better.

"Magical," she repeats and I watch her. I watch Toy

talking. She tips her head to the left and gestures with the pipe. She pauses to smoke from it. She looks at the statue of Theodore Roosevelt on the horse. Finn and Viv. She has much to say about Finn and Viv.

# josh

**W**e're in the big chairs. Josh sitting, and me perched on the arm opposite. He expected this, he says. He understands. You have to do what you have to do, he says. But that's all. Josh is not a fighter. Has he ever fought for anything? Things happen to him.

"Someday you won't even remember me," he says.

"I love you," I say. But I don't need him anymore and he knows that.

"I've always loved you," he says. but it doesn't sound so romantic anymore.

# mom

My mom has to cosign the lease for the apartment and I can't wait for her to see it. In the damp morning the squat brick building is waiting too. Breathing. The city streets where she used to walk with me. My hand in hers. She'll see it. I'm sure. She'll recognize it. She'll remember the blue bedroom, her foot next to mine, the tell-me-again times.

But she doesn't. The room holds its breath. She looks around. She wonders aloud what exactly I'm doing. "What are you trying to prove?" she says. Then, "I guess you're going to do what you're going to do."

I stand in the doorway and watch her. Her hair is so blond it's white, piled on top of her head. She leans against the windowsill with her back to the room.

"There isn't even a view," she says.

# leaving

Josh doesn't help me pack. He doesn't help me move. He doesn't come home for two days after I tell him and when he does come home, he steals back my fake ID. When I ask him about it he says he doesn't know what I'm talking about.

He watches me. I take the things I brought: the picture of my mom, a soft pillow, my down comforter. His apartment is that much emptier. He sits on the unmade bed drumming the bedside table with his long fingers. He tells me a story, one I've heard before and I already know how it ends. When I roll up the comforter and put it in a big plastic bag, I ask him if he has anything, another blanket or something to keep him warm.

"Don't worry about me," he says.

Miguel from the cafe helps me move in a truck that he borrows from his brother. I take him out to burgers and milkshakes to thank him and he tries to kiss me. I don't mind but I turn my face a little and he catches my chin with his lips.

# floating

My new window looks out at a brick wall and when it's wet I'll know it's raining. I walk around the apartment touching the walls and hanging my clothes in the little closet. I buy blue paint. I wear the overalls that Toy and I bought at Salvation Army with a bandana over my hair and a thin white tank top underneath. I borrow a stepladder from the manager who says I have to paint the walls again when I leave. It's the color of my dreams, I tell Toy in my head. I paint all four walls and carefully trim the edges. There's paint drying on my arms and some on my face. I lie down on the mattress I bought for ninety-five dollars plus fifteen to have it delivered. I'm drifting in the blue room. My bed is a cloud, a forest, a spaceship. It's a cocoon. I spread out like a five-pointed star and stare at the ceiling.

When I wake up it's dark. Pink Floyd is playing on the radio. I run a bath, leave my clothes in a pile on the floor and get in. The bathroom ceiling is strangely high and the room's painted a pale green. Not just the bath, but the whole room feels like it's underwater.

I submerge and the lip of the water pulls at my face. My toes stick out. My kneecaps. The bottom of my rib cage. Floating. When I raise my head a little I can hear the radio. I open my eyes. The room is a warm watery green.

After the bath I put on a full length, Marilyn Monroe–type satin nightgown that Toy and I bought at Community Thrift. It's black and smooth over my stomach. The apartment's cold so I wear it with wool socks and my lace-up boots, unlaced. Over it, I wear the men's plaid Pendleton shirt that Josh gave me.

Cross-legged on the mattress with a pile of fashion magazines and an old film playing silently on the TV like moving wallpaper, I tear out a picture of a girl who's appearing from the shadows. Slats of bright yellow light fall on the planes of her face, hair, cheek, chin, as she emerges from night and morning breaks through an unseen window. She's looking at someone who isn't visible, but I can tell from the curve of her eyes that she's looking at someone who's looking back at her. There's a glimpse of her bare shoulder, but her body's in darkness. She's not alone. She's waiting for the day to begin. I trim the rough edge of the page and tack the picture to my wall above the bed.

146

# imogen

I wake up in the blue room. Sheet warm and drifting in the middle of the bed. I know exactly where I am. I bathe and dress in the underwater bathroom. Brew coffee in my little coffeepot. My walk to work is through the park blocks. Past college students and the Safeway and Theodore Roosevelt Rough Rider. Miguel teases me about living alone.

"You need a husband," he says.

In the afternoon I return home through the park blocks to my stacks of magazines with their pictures of girls in summer dresses. My piles of clothes on the floor. I take off my jacket and rest it on the back of the white wooden chair that I bought at Goodwill and carried home on the bus.

At the thrift store I find a pale blue cotton fabric and make curtains for the apartment. It takes me three nights to finish them and the fabric hangs straight down to the floor. It's getting warmer and when I leave the windows open the curtains wave into the room and the sound from the street is restless and patterned like music. The dream hasn't returned since the abortion and when I go back for my checkup Jane isn't there because she had the baby.

"What did she name her?" I ask.

"Imogen," the nurse says. "Isn't that unusual?"

# toy

Imogen. I walk home from the clinic in the warm damp evening air listening to the slap of my boots on the concrete. I stop at Safeway to call Toy and she answers right away.

"Come over," I say and she says she will. The sky grows heavy and sunset-streaked on my walk home.

She arrives wearing a wide-brimmed hat, a flowered dress, the denim jacket and perfume that immediately colonizes the apartment. It smells like her mom.

"Finn gave it to me," she says.

"Do you like it?"

"Of course I do," she says. "I love it."

She twirls around the small room, takes off her sandals and hands me the hat. I put it on and go to the bathroom to look. I like the way it hides my eyes and makes me look older. Mysterious. Toy looks over my shoulder. I lift one corner and meet her eyes in the mirror. I'm looking for the part of her that feels what I feel. She's looking too. She reads my face, measures my eyes, traces my bones and brow.

"Let me do your makeup," she says. And she goes back into the blue room for her bag. I sit on my wooden chair in the tiny bathroom and face her. She outlines my eyes in black liner. Applies a pale gold eye shadow and heavy red lipstick. This is how we are when we don't need anyone else.

I put on a new dress she brought. Strapless with a T-shirt underneath and high-heeled boots and thick socks. I put on long gloves and lots of necklaces. Chains and pearls. Over it I start to put on a men's tuxedo jacket with shiny lapels, but Toy jumps up and grabs it out of my hands. She's never seen it before. She puts it on over her flowered dress and vows never to give it back.

She puts on my moccasins, my long hippy beads, and takes back the hat. We march around the room. Then we sit in the tiny kitchen, she in the white chair and me on a stool. We're smoking pot and drinking coffee. We get very serious. She leafs through a stack of pictures I've torn from magazines and makes two piles.

"These I love," she says. "These I hate." In the pile of pictures she loves there's a skinny girl whose makeup looks like bruises. I know that summer's coming and Toy will sit in her mom's backyard next to the empty pool and watch her pale legs turn red in the sun.

She points at the skinny girl with the blank expression. "See how she looks," she says. "She looks like me."

Sometimes everything bubbles up in me and I want her to know that I know. That I know what it's like.

How it is with her mom. That I know that she wakes her mom up and tries to get her to eat. That her mom gets dressed in the afternoon, puts on the makeup and the dresses that she wore when she was married. That she drinks white wine and watches herself in the mirror before falling asleep again, fully dressed, in her unmade bed. I want Toy to know that I know. That no matter how many boys tell her they love her, how many boys tell her she's beautiful, how many boys crawl into her window at night and make love to her, it doesn't help. That I know it doesn't help. She is my sister and I love her. Like I want her to love me.

Instead, I look through the stack of pictures she loves. I find one of a girl whose face is full to the camera. She's squinting through big sunglasses and holding her wide round hat down close on her head. Her smile is generous beneath the dark thick glasses.

"This is what you look like to me," I say. "Beautiful."

# a raft on the ocean

Toy is my family. Our story goes something like this: I have a blue bedroom in the city and sometimes I sleep in the middle of my bed, all spread out. And sometimes Toy comes over and she sleeps on one side, on her stomach and when she has bad dreams she wakes me up.

"Anna?" she says.

And I say, "I'm here." And then she goes back to sleep.

# summer

When Toy leaves the next night and I'm alone again, I make a box of macaroni and cheese. Above the stove I've taped a large black-and-white photograph of a family ripped from a magazine. They tumble out of an oversized beach house, everyone laughing and dogs running around the edges. Sometimes I count the people in the photograph. Kids and grandparents and aunts and uncles. People in between. There's a girl my age in faded jeans and bare feet. It's summer and the photograph is filled with light.

The girl smiles up at an older woman, a mother or an aunt, and the woman smiles back at her. The water for the macaroni comes to a boil. I look at the family, each one touching another one. Some casually on the shoulder or with their arms around another one. I strain the macaroni and mix it with the orange powder, the butter and the milk. Another girl, a younger one, squints into the sun. I take my dinner to the bed and turn on the TV. When I'm done I carry the bowl to the sink and turn out the light but leave the TV on for company. I lie in bed listening to the voices on the television until I fall asleep.

# sam

Sometimes kids come into the cafe after school and sometimes I'm invisible to them. I want someone to ask me why I'm there. Why I'm not in school. I want someone to recognize that I'm a kid just like they are.

And then Sam does. He's a skinny boy with hair in his eyes studying with three other kids.

"Hey."

"Hey."

"Do you work here?" he says but then he laughs because I'm behind the counter wearing an apron and making a hot chocolate that he ordered.

After a while. "Hey," he says again.

"Hey," I say, but quietly, so he can't hear it above the espresso machine. His friends are all sitting at a table, thick, highlighted books open in front of them.

Before he leaves he comes back again. "I'm Sam," he says and he holds out his hand. I wipe mine on my apron and then take his.

"I'm Anna."

# the river

Saturday. No Toy. She hasn't been back for days. She doesn't answer the phone. I get dressed and it's getting warmer and it's easier, I think, to be in the city without Toy. I get to be the girl in the black dress. I get to be the romantic one with nobody to contradict me. No best friend to remind me of what I'm not.

Finally, Sunday. My date with Sam. The stores are closed and the sidewalk is empty. Nobody sees me. I pass the liquor store, the grocery store, the park blocks. I pass office buildings, ivy-covered restaurants, boarded-up strip clubs. Down by the water, it's as if I have the river to myself. I lean over the railing, looking at the muddy gray.

"Anna," I imagine him saying it. I imagine how I look, leaning over the railing with the sun warming the backs of my calves like a blush. I'm wearing the black dress and black Converse and I have a sweatshirt tied around my waist. One leg kicks up as I lean over. The dress rises in the back and my hair falls forward. I try to hold the position, because I can imagine how it looks like I'm falling, but I'm not.

I lift both feet from the ground and think about the picture of Toy dropping from the sky.

"Anna," he says and this time it's for real. He stands behind me, looking past me at the indeterminate color of the river. The sun is still unfamiliar and I slide down, turn around, and squint.

"Sam," I say. We made a date, but I guess I thought he wouldn't come. His eyes flicker and stop on mine. He has little crinkles when he smiles. He's smiling and so am I.

Suddenly the park is full of people, joggers and children and dogs. We get spare changed, we get busked. We don't know what to say. Sam is my age and that makes him seem so young. But he's tall, really tall, and floppy and his hands are large.

We lean together against the railing over the slow-moving river. Now I'm a character in a black-and-white movie, a working girl out with her boy on the waterfront. I'm sixteen years old and Sam and I wear identical black Converse. I can feel my face crinkling too.

"Anna?" Sam says.

"What?"

"Nothing," he says. And then he says it again. "Anna?"

"What?"

"Nothing."

We walk to the end of the park and down the steps to

the water. A dead fish, larger than any fish I've ever seen, rotting. A tire. Three plastic bottles, one Coke, two water, bobbing. Sam takes off his jacket and spreads it out on the dock. I sit cross-legged, leaning forward. The sun casts out over the river and Sam sits cross-legged too, leaning back on his hands.

He admires my skin in the deep V in the back of the dress, then leans forward and touches it, lightly. His touch startles me. I don't expect it. I don't know what to expect. He touches me, then stops and leans back. Just enough.

He's looking at the water and he's looking at me. I'm talking about the stepbrothers. I have funny stories about the stepbrothers.

"Where are they now?" he asks and I say I don't know. They left when their father left. All that's left, I say, is a pair of perfectly broken-in Levi's.

"My favorite jeans," I say and we talk about his family. His mom and dad and little sister and older brother. They live at the edge of downtown in a cluster of old Victorian houses. Not that far from my apartment.

"Come to dinner," he says and I picture me with his family around a big table, napkins in our laps. What would we talk about? What would they think of me? I don't know about parents, I think. Self-conscious now, I sit up straighter and look at him. Does he really want me to meet his family? My cheeks are sun-flushed and tight. Sam smiles into my face and says that he's hungry, that everybody would be happy to meet me.

"I can't," I say. But it doesn't hold up.

"Why not?" he asks.

And by the time the sun has leaned into the distance, I'm walking to his house.

# a real family

Sam's house is everything I wanted, but didn't know to want.

"I'm home," he calls, pushing open the heavy wooden door with me close behind. Past him, worn hardwood floors stretch through archways into a patchwork of deeply colored rugs. The house thrums with the smell of roasting meat, the murmur of voices, rustling movement. There are thick curtains in muted patterns draping the windows and sheltering Sam's family from the city outside.

I want to wrap myself in this house like a blanket.

Instinctively I take Sam's hand and then, just as quickly, I drop it. He keeps walking but I'm still in the entry, fixed in front of a wall of framed family pictures. Dozens of them: here is Sam and a similarly featured little sister; a solemn and masculine brother; and the mother, casual, relaxed and happy. Here is a bookish bearded father. Black-and-white. Color. The house is warm and I feel flushed. This home pulses with their shared life. I don't belong here. I turn to leave, but Sam puts his hand against my back.

160

"Look, this is when I was three." He points to a picture of a squirming boy in his mother's lap. Her arms tight around him. But I'm caught by another picture. A shot of them all together. A composite of kindred features, like a repeating theme of crinkly smiles. A moment, a little blurry of everyone looking in one direction, at something that's happening off-camera, everyone laughing and leaning against everyone else.

"I have to go," I say, but it comes out in a whisper and when I look up, Sam's mom is standing in front of me.

"Hello," she says, holding out her hand. She wears no makeup, and looks at me with honest, even eyes. Gray mixes with blond in her hair. She gives me a strong handshake.

"Hi."

"Mom, this is Anna," Sam says. "Can she stay for dinner?"

"Sure, Anna." She looks at me. "Do your folks know you're here?" she asks. And of course I have nothing to say to that.

# dinner

We're upstairs in Sam's bedroom. He leaves the door open. Here are a lifetime of interests: posters of the night sky, an electric guitar, a skateboard, piles of books and magazines. He has heavy wooden furniture. Adult furniture. Solid. He has a bed with a headboard and a desk with a matching chair.

"My grandparents," he says, meaning the furniture. I sit down at his desk and look through his school books. I can see Sam at the center of his life. Connected.

Hours earlier he kissed me, just lightly, catching me unaware as I studied the river. He doesn't kiss me now, but leans against the bed, watching me.

"Hungry?" he asks, and I am. His dad steps into the doorway.

"Dinner's ready."

Sam's family tumbles out of their rooms to the kitchen. Everyone's talking at once. We each carry a dish to the dining room, mashed potatoes with bits of skin; a crusty steak cut in long strips, showing red in the middle; green beens with bell peppers, everything in rough heavy dishes. Sam points to a pitcher of water and I carry that. He carries the beans and his older brother grabs a stack of mismatched cloth napkins and a handful of silverware. Sam's father takes off his apron and sighs.

"That's that," he says.

I sit next to Sam and his brother reaches across the table and shakes my hand.

"I'm Mark," he says and then they all start talking. Sam's sister tells a story about three girls from school. Nobody likes them.

"What does that mean, nobody likes them?" her father asks. Sam's mom, in a soft shirt and faded jeans, talks to Mark about his car.

"How much work does it need?" she asks.

Sam explains to his dad about the three girls and his voice combines with the others. Rising and falling with the sounds of the silverware. I arrange the slivers of steak around the mashed potatoes and the green beans. It's all so good. I keep stretching to take another piece of steak or spoon of potatoes and Sam's mom looks over and smiles. Then she turns back to say something about Mark's transmission.

I look at each of them, from one to another, puzzling over their similarity. I measure their features, their expressions, their posture. I can't place it. And then I do. They dress alike. Like a tribe. Not in the same clothes or the same fabrics, but everything fits the same way, layers in the same way, there's an unconscious way of combining color so that I might recognize them as a family even if I just saw their laundry piled together.

Sam wears a blue T-shirt with a worn neck and a plaid shirt that I find out later is his brother's. I'm tracing how Sam's curls are the twins of his sister's when she stops talking and looks at me.

"I like your dress," she says and I blush even though Toy and I always say that nothing can make me blush. It's the black dress, of course, and I have a necklace made out of a chain and a bit of frayed black ribbon. Everyone turns to look at me and I get so hot that I'm sure my chest, framed by the square neckline, is bright red.

"It's from the sixties, isn't it?" Sam's mom says. "I love those dresses, they're so pretty." She turns to her daughter. "I think I have one, Em," she says. "You should look and see if it fits you."

"It's pretty," Sam says, looking at me, crinkling. Mark looks at me and the dress, and then turns back to his dad and asks something about the car.


Sam walks me home like it's a real date. Kisses me at the door to my apartment building. I wear his jean jacket to stay warm and he lets me keep it. I lean against his chest, close my eyes, and picture how we look, silhouetted against the brick building. I save every second to tell

Toy. Now I have a romantic story that rivals hers. Sam's gone all week, it's Spring Break, but he promises to meet me next Monday, after I get off work and he gets out of school.

Monday feels too far away, but I don't say that.

"Bye," he says.

"Bye," I say and I go up to my apartment and turn on the lights. I turn on the TV so the room will be filled with voices. I take off the black dress and hang it from a hook on the wall. It's dark outside and my little apartment is warm and full of light. I listen to the TV and watch the dress until I fall asleep.

# where i belong

**W**hen I wake up in the morning, at first I can't tell what's different. And then I remember. Sam's family. The sound of silverware against plates and talking and everyone asking questions and interrupting. And the way sometimes I forgot and it felt like I belonged there. The parts that I forgot to remember to tell Toy. The worn cloth napkins and how everyone carried their dish to the sink and how Sam and I washed and Em, Sam's sister, dried.

I scrub my face clean and wear a striped shirt like Jean Seberg with skinny jeans and flat shoes and I curl my eyelashes and wear mascara and my cheeks are pink and my hair is light and curls slightly and hangs in my eyes and I know. I know that everyone else will see it too. I wear Sam's jacket and a cotton scarf and I storm through the park blocks. The cherry blossoms rage around me. And when I get to work, cappuccinos are made! Lattes! The tea is piping hot! Miguel is singing and my apron is tight around my waist and even the women with painted nails leave me a tip.

I replay the day with Sam. I can see us stretching into the future, me in his jacket and his arm around my shoulders. I'm bursting. I call Toy after work and the phone just rings and rings. I walk down to the river where Sam kissed me and I stare at the water. I find a pay phone and call Toy again. Nothing. I walk over to the train station and back up to my apartment as the sky gets soft and dark and the warm spring rain starts.

The city, I remember, is full of possibilities.

Back in the apartment the black dress still hangs on the wall and the pictures of girls in summer dresses gaze at me, their faces turned toward the light.

But it's early and there's only Top Ramen to eat. I go back out to the pay phone and try calling Toy again. Nothing. I hang up and then I call again. And then I hang up and call again. But no one answers.

I call my mom, but she doesn't answer either. I rest my forehead against the earpiece. It's dark outside and I go back to my apartment and think about Sam's house. I turn on all the lights and the TV and I boil water for tea and I draw a bath, but I don't get in.


The next morning I'm back at the cafe. I wish it wasn't Spring Break and that Sam would come after school. Just surprise me, like he couldn't wait to see me. I imagine hearing him say, "Hey." And turning and seeing him standing there. I turn the image over like a secret stone.

Sometimes it's like nobody sees me. Like these women order without ever meeting my eyes. "A latte," they say and tap their nails on the glass, studying the backs of their hands.

All day long, these women order their drinks without ever seeing me. And then one does. She looks me straight in the eye and then up and down.

"Anna?" she says. She's a friend of my mom's. "How's your mom?" she asks. "Still married to—?" She digs around in her purse. She doesn't ask why I'm working here. "I'll have a cappuccino," she says. "I'm in a hurry."

# a boy

That night I walk to Josh's apartment. I don't want him anymore, but I'm standing beneath his window and his lights are off and I wonder if he's there. I wonder if he's alone. I walk to the bar and look in through the yellow windows. I don't go home. I'm following my own footfall and the city is empty.

Burnside, Couch, Davis, I cross through the empty streets. I go to Little Birds cafe and meet a boy. I'm impatient. Restless. Like I'm wearing my nerves on the outside. After a while we go to his apartment to drink. We have sex. He gets a rubber and I put it on him. I'm naked but he won't take off his shirt.

"Take off your shirt," I tell him. I feel very experienced. I'm on top of him, rocking my hips back and forth and I yank at the shirt. I ignore his hands pulling it down.

"Stop," he says and I ignore him. His chest is covered with dozens of angry pimples, a mountain range of inflamed whiteheads. He won't look at me and I drop the shirt. We roll over, so he's on top of me, and I stare over his shoulder at the empty wall until he comes.

# the empty apartment

I walk back to my apartment. It's late and I walk in the middle of the street where there are no shadows. In the dim rooms, I can make out Sam's jacket on the back of my small wooden chair. I don't think about the boy from the cafe. I decide it didn't happen.

I take off my clothes and lay under my comforter, but I'm unable to sleep.

# beginning to get the hang of it

Then it's Monday and Sam's standing in my apartment. I know how bare it must seem. How hurried. Like a girl half-dressed. He walks through the kitchen and stops in the tiny bathroom. I stand next to him and we look up at the water stains on the tall ceilings. Back in my room he looks at the small TV, my mattress on the floor, my piles of clothes and the small wooden chair. He looks out the window at the brick wall and when he turns he sees the black dress hanging on the wall. He relaxes.

"Is that the dress?" he says and walks over. He feels the hem between his thumb and forefinger, then he sees the picture of the two girls. The one in the green skirt stares straight at him.

"Do you know her?" he asks, not understanding. And then seeing the other pictures, he steps back and takes them in.

"Oh," he says and he holds out his hand for mine. We look at the pictures together.

"This is my favorite," I say, motioning to a girl with

hair in her eyes. Sam points to another, a boy and girl on a couch, kissing.

I look. The girl's hair obscures their faces, but I can see the angle of the boy's jaw. The way he encircles her in his arms. I can tell there's something formal about this moment. Something important. Sam sees it too because he turns and faces me and without letting go of my hand, he tips his head and kisses me. I tip my head and kiss him. It's our second kiss, but our first real kiss and I see that there's something here, something important.

I tell myself the story of the kiss. How we meet. How he kisses me. How he tips his head. We kiss and I tell myself the story of the kiss. How he holds my hand. It's a long kiss. We stand so close to the wall that I can put my hand out and touch it. I lean into him. I'm at home in the still apartment. We close our eyes against the dusty light. There's a burnt smell. A low hum comes from the refrigerator and, at intervals, street sounds penetrate. Faint sirens, then nothing. It's a good long kiss.

After some time I forget to narrate the kiss. I can hear a bus sighing at the stop near my window and the cars stopping and starting with the traffic light. I can hear the familiar hum of the refrigerator. I put one hand out and touch the wall. I remember to not think about the boy from Little Birds cafe. I remember that in this story it didn't happen.

Sam pulls away. He's talking about dinner. I'm in-

vited to his house again, he says. His mom likes me. His
sister too.

"Yeah. My mom"—he steps closer so I can feel his
breath on my cheek—"was shocked." I turn my mouth
close to his.

"That I live alone?" I say.

"Yeah. But really," he says, "she wants to know what
you eat." We both look toward the kitchen. I realize the
burnt smell is the coffeepot left on.

He follows me in and I turn the coffeemaker off. I
wave at the boxes on the counter. "Macaroni and cheese,"
I say. "Three for a dollar."


On Fridays the kids cook the whole meal. I help them
broil salmon, steam broccoli and make rice. You don't
stir rice, I learn, and you have to time the broccoli or it
gets mushy. Mark rubs the fish with spices. Em cleans
the berries for dessert. I've never seen kids cook before,
except Toy because her mom's drunk, but she only ever
makes scrambled eggs and toast. Em checks her brother's
work and when they tease her, I want to close my eyes
and pretend it's me.

I break a glass. Mark and Sam just laugh. Em makes a
big show out of telling me it doesn't matter. I'm given the
water pitcher and sent to the table. It's their way of telling
me I can still be trusted. Alone in the dining room I listen to their muffled voices through the swinging door.

There are cut branches in a vase on the table. A woven runner. One of the bulbs is out in the chandelier. I straighten each fork, each knife, on the folded napkins.

Later I'm staring at Sam and his dad, comparing their cheekbones.

"Do you go to school?" Sam's mom tries to make the question sound nonchalant, like she hadn't been waiting to ask. She wears the same oversized gingham shirt, rolled at the cuffs, and there's no jewelry on her hands.

Sam and Em turn to me when their mom asks the question and Sam says, "Mom." Like he's already asked her not to start.

No, I want to say, I don't go to school. I'm the girl who works in a cafe. The girl behind the counter. I'm the black dress and worn sneakers. I'm tips in a tip jar. I'm a five-pointed star. I'm the four walls of my apartment. The girl in the abortion clinic. I'm the one wandering through the city looking for something.

Yes, I dropped out of school.

And then suddenly I am so angry. I want my own big brother, my own little sister, my own mom in rolled-up shirtsleeves. I want my own father. He'd be a ferocious listener. A lean-forward-on-his-elbows-and-never-interrupt father. I want to be Sam. I want his life. I would do everything right. I would go to school. I would be a virgin. I would learn to make mashed potatoes with cream and butter. I would set the table every night.

I meet Sam's mom's even gaze. I'm glad she asked, but I don't know what to say.

"No," I say and then I compliment her on something, which always works with my mom.

"That's a beautiful vase," I say, but she just looks at me. Her eyes hold mine. She knows exactly what I'm doing.

After dinner, Mark and Em and Sam teach me to play poker. They bet Matchbox cars and Em and Sam cheat. We're in the family room together listening to Mark's music. After dessert we clear the table and wash the dishes. I'm beginning to get the hang of it.

# sam's girlfriend

**S**am's a virgin. We wait. We have dinner at his house, we go to the river. We lean over the railing and watch the water and he rests his hand on the back of my neck. I borrow his jean jacket, then give it back, then borrow it again. I grow impatient.

"Slow down," he says.

"But Sam," I say.

"But Anna," he says.

"But," I say. "But, but, but," but then he holds me in a way that makes me laugh. He's very serious. He never jokes about sex.

He takes my hand and says things like, "I like this moment, right here." And then he kisses me, "and this one." And then he kisses me again, "and this one." My hands reach up under the front of his shirt. Down the back of his pants, under his belt. I love the way he smells and the way he looks at me and the way he smooths the hair away from my face. He knows I'm not a virgin.

"I know, Anna," he says and there's a way he seems older than me. Like he knows what he wants. He comes by the cafe after school and sits at a table where he says he can watch me, but when I look up he's doing his homework, his face crinkling in concentration.

Sometimes we go to his house and our only touch is a look. It's the way, I think, he looks at me. And I lose myself in the sounds of his family, the music on the stereo, his sister calling for his dad, his dad taking off his apron and sighing. Sam tells me about his classes. We make plans to meet his friends. I am learning something, I think, but I don't know what it is.

Then suddenly it's a hot day and we're at my apartment and my dress is off and nobody is saying "but." He's not saying "slow down." He's looking at me and we can't wait. We can't help ourselves. He's everywhere. He takes my nose, my ear, my whole breast in his mouth. He slides his hand under my arm and between my fingers. He feels the bones down my chest and cups the skin on my stomach. We're on my bed. It's so early that without any lights, my room is bright and he can see everything. He touches every part of the front of me and then turns me over and touches every part of the back of me. He feels in between my toes. We have sex again and again and again. He's always ready.

Afterward we take a shower and get dressed. He dries his hair with his fingers. I follow him home for dinner.

In the blocks between his house and my apartment, everything changes. I want it to change. I want to be less like me. Less like the girl in that story. I don't want to be the girl who's always looking. The one who has no mother, the one who has no father.

I want to be like any other girl. I want to be Sam's girlfriend. A girl who washes the spinach and removes the stems, who fills the water pitcher and sets the table, who sits down and waits for everyone else to start eating.

The afternoon air cools me on the way to Sam's house. It soothes the flush of my face. My swollen lips.

Sam's mom paces herself, asking only a few questions and saving some for next time. What do I do to make money? What do I want to do? And then the next night, Do I want to go to college? And another: What about my mom? Doesn't she worry? Doesn't she think it's dangerous to live alone?

I think she worries that Em will think I'm romantic. That it's romantic to drop out of school, to live alone. Em loves my dresses and each night I wear a different one for her: the blue cotton one, a green silk one, a bohemian print. After dinner I look through Em's closet and we pick out outfits for her: a gray cardigan with a yellow T-shirt and blue cotton pants; or a red-and-white-striped long-sleeved T-shirt with blue jeans, blue sneakers and a yellow raincoat.

"Sam's lucky," she says, meaning me.

"Yes," I say, meaning all of them. Meaning the sounds her family makes from the next room.

In her bedroom, on one wall, is a group of paintings that Sam's mom made in college. Big, brightly colored still life paintings of eggplants and grapes, wooden bowls and a chipped ceramic pitcher. Em and I look at them. She imagines that the eggplant became eggplant parmigiana on her parents' first date.

"They fell in love at college," she says and she sighs. Em is a romantic girl. She has pictures of her mom and her dad together when they were young, pinned to her wall. We look at them. I look at the jar of cherry blossom branches on her bedside table. Her mom cut them from a tree in the backyard. I find myself closing my eyes and wishing so hard. Maybe she would cut some for me, I think.

# the wrong way down
# a one-way street

**S**am has midterms and it's been three days since I've seen him. I can't reach Toy. I wander from one end of town to the other, but I avoid Little Birds cafe. I deposit my tips in the bank on Fifth Street and walk from one side of town to the other until it gets dark and then I walk home again. I know how to walk through the city at night, purposefully, in the middle of the street and against traffic, away from parked cars where someone could be hiding. Josh taught me that.

"Walk the wrong way down a one-way street," he told me. Make sure there's no one around before you bring out your keys. Always lock the door to your apartment when you go down to the laundry room. And never, ever buzz anyone in, unless you're sure who they are.

"Always wear your purse strapped against your body," he'd say. "They don't teach you that in the suburbs."

"At least he's making himself useful," my mom said.

So I'm alert to danger. I scan the street for moving shadows. I avoid dark doorways and groups of men standing together. I walk with my shoulders back and my arms swinging.

And I miss Sam. I leave work around four in the afternoon. It's still bright daylight and because it's warmed up and the sky has cleared, I'm already sweating in my thin sweater. I walk past Urban Middle School, where Sam went to school. Where Em is going now. School's letting out and the girls and boys clump together in little groups, carrying backpacks like afterthoughts.

It looks like my middle school and there's even the lone kid, books clutched to her chest, who might have been me. I watch her thread through the clusters of students, pass through the gate and walk down the way I'm walking. I follow a bit behind. She walks fast but I have nowhere to go, the evening yawns out in front of me, so I walk slowly letting the distance between us grow.

The sun is on my face and I'm thinking about nothing at all.

About half a block past the school I hear a knocking. A rhythmic tapping and I look at the building I'm passing and then into the street where the cars are rushing by. I look all around and the tapping continues and then I see him, knuckles against the window, in a parked car by the sidewalk.

He's sitting in the passenger seat. He's skinny and white and not wearing any pants. His hand tugs at his penis. He stares at me with wet eyes and an open mouth and he's not smiling, but I can see his gums. He's searching out my eyes and for a second I look right at him. Then I look away. I walk faster. I feel a floodrush of nausea, like something rotten is stuck in my throat. I try to swallow past it. The feeling chases me back to my apartment. The street is empty, but I look around before unlocking the front door to my building.

# sam

At Sam's house I become the garlic bread maker. I'm responsible for slicing and buttering, for wielding the garlic press, for keeping an eye on the broiler. Sam teaches me how to cut and steam the green beans and Em shows me how to slice a bell pepper. I fill pitchers with water and carry them to the table.

I watch Sam's dad sauté garlic, blanch tomatoes and simmer pasta sauce. I eat at Sam's house three nights a week. I have my own seat at the table.

On the other days I experiment with feeding myself at home. I make small salads and dress them in oil and vinegar. I buy a floral apron at the thrift store and a set of wood-handled knives. Sam and I make love.

We have ninety minutes between when I get off work and when he's expected home. We have all day on the weekends. It's nearly summer now and Sam likes to take off my shorts and my underwear and leave on my T-shirt. I like to wear his shirt with nothing underneath and we like to have sex and then make toast with lots of butter on it, eat it, and then have sex again. Sam circles my legs with his and locks his ankles together. He rubs my cheekbones. He closes his eyes when he comes.

# mom

I'm so happy I forget to wonder about Toy. I forget to count the days since I last heard from her. I forget to remember things to tell her. I stop thinking about the dream and I almost believe the boy from Little Birds cafe never happened. I don't wander the streets of Portland after work anymore or stop outside Josh's apartment and look to see if the light is on. I spend my afternoons with Sam or I go home and make little dinners. I take baths and listen to music. I cut out pictures of magazines and pin them to the walls.

I don't call my mom. She calls the cafe sounding angry. She says it's been more than a month and she's been worried. It's been two months. More than two months. And she hasn't worried or she'd know that. I make a dinner date with her for the next night. She's only in town for a few days, she says.

In the restaurant I order pasta and a salad and she looks surprised.

"I could never get you to eat a salad," she says.

"Did you try?"

"Of course I tried," she says. "You were such a fussy eater."

"I've been learning to cook," I say.

"In that tiny kitchen?" she says. Then she gets to her point. "I think this little experiment has gone on long enough. I think it's time for you to come home." She looks at me, finishes her glass of wine and motions for the waiter. The lighting is not kind to my mom. Her face has settled. She tells me about the man she's dating and I picture him with a thick carpet of hair and hacking morning cough. He's shocked that she lets me live alone in the city. He'd looked at her like she's a bad mother. Now she's taking control. I'm going to come home, she says.

"You are my daughter after all." Our salads arrive. I listen. I don't argue. I wish I could tell her how it is for me.

I could go to a new high school, she tells me, a private school. I'll live at home. We'll recarpet the downstairs. Do I have a boyfriend? "I'd like to meet him," she says. She motions for the waiter and he brings her another glass of wine. Her face becomes animated. Her boyfriend has a house on the coast. We can go together. Meet his children. "The coast is beautiful this time of year," she says.

He has two daughters and a son. They're very close.

When we're done with the salads, the pasta arrives. Would I prefer to move upstairs? I could redecorate my old bedroom. Of course we'll move when she gets married again. More wine.

The abortion: Did I go to my follow-up appointment? Is everything alright? Will I be able to have children? Do I ever see Josh anymore?

"What a loser he turned out to be," she says. Good-looking, though. Even she could see that. Young women have it tough. Pregnancy, birth control, marriage—no upside for young women at all. Even worse in her day. She got pregnant young too. Miscarried. Wasn't sure she could even have kids. Surprised when she was pregnant with me. She wanted a baby, she says. She'd been so lonely.

"It's difficult, though, meeting men with a small child." Getting married with a young daughter. "And being a stepmother? The worst." I shouldn't marry a man with kids, she says. This she says emphatically. "Don't marry a man with kids, Anna. It's a burden. Too much of a burden." She finishes her wine. "And relationships are hard enough without it."

"What about my dad?" I ask. It isn't like I never asked before.

"That was my mistake, Anna," she says. She always says that. And then she says, "He was useless." She always says that too. And then, a pause. "But he gave me you."

The dinner is over. She shrugs on her sweater and says that she's OK to drive. I say I'll think about it.

She looks at me. "You've gained a little weight," she says. But it looks good, she says. Not to worry.

# sam's mom

Sam's mom asks to talk to me privately after dinner and I'm sure it's about sex. I'm sure she sees it or senses it or smells it on us. It's like a fog that envelopes us. She pulls her chair back from the dining room table and asks me to follow her and in that moment, looking at her, I realize that Sam and I could have waited. He would still be a virgin and it would be worth it, I think, to not have to lie. To not have to have this conversation. To not have to sit in her office waiting for her to say something. But then I think about all of the warm corners of Sam's body and how I know each one. And how different it would be if I didn't know him like that. I sit in a stiff chair and look at the floor.

"Anna," she says. "I'm worried about you."

She looks like Jane, just then. Like she would stay with me and listen to me and not leave until I ran out of things to say. And she's comfortable with silence. She simply watches me when I have nothing to say. She doesn't struggle to fill the space. In my head, I'm trying out the stories I could tell her.

I live in a blue room, I could say. And I don't know what comes next.

Her cheeks are red from being in the garden. "We love having you here," she says. "Em and Sam love your company."

At Sam's name I get nervous again. I look at the ground.

Sam's parents think he's a virgin. When they came to his room to talk to him about me, he lied. He lied and they believed him. "We understand," they'd said. "What it's like." How it is. How much he likes me and how easy it would be. "But sex," they'd said, "is a responsibility." A responsibility Sam isn't ready for. So he lied.

"We're waiting," he'd told them.

Then, according to Sam, his mom had said how smart she thinks I am. How strong. How I could do anything.

And that's what she's saying now. "You're so smart, Anna," she says. "You could do anything." Her face is lined and her hair is brown with threads of gray. She tucks a piece behind her ear like a girl. She doesn't wear any makeup and when she looks at me her eyes are wide open. Her eyelashes are so faint, I can barely see them.

I think how different she is from my mom. From Toy's mom. When she says I can do anything, she doesn't mean a boy, a boyfriend, a husband. She means me. Me. I could do anything. I don't know what to say. I can't concentrate when she says these things.

I think about climbing into Sam's mom's skin and

wearing her blue shirt and living in her wooden house. I'd garden and read thick books about history. I'd paint and work and write. My husband would bake bread. My daughter would want to be an artist. I'd tuck my hair behind my ears. I'd have two sons. I'd wonder if they were keeping secrets from me.

She's still watching me and I know that she expects some kind of response. I swallow. I make my eyes round.

"Thank you," I say.

"Anna, what you're doing is hard," she says. "You're not supposed to have to do it on your own, you know." She looks at me hard. "You don't have to do it alone," she says.

"Thank you," I say again.

# sam

Sam stands at my window looking out at the redbrick wall. He's naked and holds his penis idly in one hand. I'm still on the mattress, naked too, but wrapped in sheets. I had an orgasm when he rubbed me with his fingers and he watches me with his eyes round and his mouth a little open. Surprised by the suddenness of it. He goes to get a glass of water and comes back to the bed. He unwraps me from the sheet and follows the curves of my legs with the tips of his fingers. He's surprised how easy it is. He's surprised that a girl wants to have sex with him. But I'm not surprised. I'm thinking about what his mom said.

"Sex is the easy part," I tell him, looking out the useless window.

# toy

The next day Sam is dreamy and talking quietly. "It's almost like Toy is imaginary," he says. "Will I ever meet her?"

# stories

My bell rings and the walls vibrate with the sound. I run down the stairs thinking it's Sam, but a woman's figure shifts on the other side of the wavy glass. Sam's mom, I think. Or Jane? But I haven't seen Jane since the abortion. I pull on the heavy door and the woman turns toward me. It's my mom in her yellow dress with a sweater wrapped tight around her. She looks unfamiliar on my worn steps. The traffic moves relentlessly behind her.

She holds her purse in one hand, and in the other, a large shopping bag.

"Anna," she says and there's so much in my name. She puts down the shopping bag and turns away from me back toward the street. "We used to live near here, you know," she says. She seems smaller somehow and for the first time I can see that she looks like that picture, the one of her mom.

"Mom?"

"Not that far." She gestures up the street. "Only a few blocks from here." She looks off into the distance.

"Do you want to come in?" I ask.

"No, I have to go, I'm meeting Mike," she says and I don't ask who Mike is. I don't ask what happened to the other one. This is how I see my mom, how I've always seen her: coming and going. Carrying her purse. Leaving, never staying. I step out onto the landing and close the door behind me. I follow her gaze.

"What was it like?" I ask.

"I loved that apartment," she says.

I look at her. "I thought you hated being alone," I say and she laughs.

"I was never alone," she says. "You had your own room, but you always slept with me."

"I remember that," I say. "You used to bundle me up in your arms when you slept."

"You fit right under my chin," she says, remembering. She puts down the shopping bag and curves her arm around my waist. "If I were stronger . . ." she says, but then she doesn't finish.

"If you were stronger?"

"I don't know. After your dad left, I guess. But you're too old for these stories." She sounds tired, but she holds me tighter.

"Mom?" I say.

"What is it?" she says and I can hear that she's prepared for anything.

"Do you think I'm strong?" I ask.

She doesn't answer right away. Then she does. "Anna,"

she says and the traffic pauses between lights. And again, there's everything there in the way she says my name. "So strong." She stops. The traffic starts up again. We're both silent and her arm is still around me. I think about our rooms, painted blue. About her, then, and me, now. "Stronger than I ever was," she says.

How would our stories be different, I think, if I asked different questions?

"Mom," I start, but she looks down at the bag.

"I got you this blanket. It's cotton, so I thought it would be good for summer," she says.

"Mom," I say again.

"I still want you to come home," she says and she hands me the shopping bag. She drops her arm, getting ready to leave.

"I know," I say.

# summer

Sam's sick. He has a high temperature, he says, and his mom's worried. He's staying home from school. He calls me at the cafe. He's all alone, he says.

"Come over." His voice is thin.

I'm making a latte for a woman in a brown linen dress and I hold the phone between my ear and my shoulder, tracing a pattern with the coffee in the milk and hand it to her. She takes a sip of the drink and sighs. She smiles at me.

"We're slow," I tell Sam. "I'll ask to leave early."

"We have hours," he says, meaning before anyone else will be home.

I change out my tips for bills and put thirty-seven dollars in my pocket. One twenty, one ten, a five and two ones. Everything's perfect. I'm wearing a red cotton sundress, white Converse sneakers and it's warm, warm, warm. The streets between the cafe and Sam's house are perfect. My anticipation is perfect. Everything happy bubbles up in me and I run my hand along brick walls and trees and lampposts. The sky is a perfect blue holding a round yellow ball and I walk past the beating roar of Ira Keller Fountain and then the university and then the streets get quieter and more residential. I feel like this day was made for me and I have somewhere to go. Somewhere to be.

Only Sam's sick. Sicker than I imagined. His face is pale and his lips are cracked. His hair sticks to his face with sweat and he looks thin in his pajamas. He scares me. He stands unsteadily in the doorway and pulls at my hand like a child. He's excited. He takes my hand in his damp one and shows me how hard he is. He kisses me with an open mouth and when I pull away I can see how glassy his eyes are. I don't recognize him.

But he leads me up the stairs. We pass through thick chunks of sunlight in the stairwell and when we get to his bedroom I start to pull back but then he kisses me until it changes and I want him as much as he wants me.

I run my fingers across his forehead, unsticking his hair. Kissing his brow, his ear, his cheekbone. I hold both of his wrists together in my hands and cover the side of his face with my breath. I want to taste him. He's pushing against me and I hold his wrists tighter and jerk him toward the bed. I like this. He's on his back and I pull off his pajama top and look down at his smooth chest. I press my cheek to his breastbone, gathering up his wrists again and holding them over his head with one hand. I press my face beneath his arm and I'm kissing him. His feverish body. I let go of his wrist and pull his pajamas down around his ankles. I lean back on my heels and pull off my dress. I put my mouth on his penis but he pulls me up and I climb off the bed. I take off my underwear and stand looking down at him. He's flushed. I lean over and kiss his mouth and he whispers things to me. He's telling me that he loves me. I push off my sneakers and my socks and climb back on the bed. I'm straddling him and fitting him inside me.

"Oh," he says. I put my weight forward on my hands and rock against him. His face is in the path of sunlight from the open window and his eyes are squeezed tightly shut against the brightness. Everything is perfect. I'm on top of him and his hands are around my waist and I feel like I could just raise my hands up to the ceiling and I do. I lift my arms straight up. The door swings open.

His mom has one hand on the doorknob, the other on a slender briefcase. She's wearing a dark-colored suit. Her hair's limp and in her eyes and she just freezes. She just stops and I think I can see us reflected in her flat brown eyes. Sam's hands are still holding my waist and I turn to him because I think that maybe he didn't hear her come in but he did. His eyes are fixed on her. And when I look back at her, her eyes are fixed on him. It's like I'm not even there.

I drop my arms.

"Sam, meet me downstairs," she says. Her eyes flicker toward me. "Anna, you can go home."

I look at Sam trembling beneath me. I don't know

what to think, because everything's changed. I can hear it in her voice and the way she turned away from me. I'm still sitting on top of him and he's sick—I know that—he's sick and trembling beneath me.

"I'm sorry," I say.

But Sam says nothing. I put on my sundress and shoes. I look around for my bag. I wonder how I could have ever felt at home here.

# toy

I go straight to a pay phone and call Toy. She answers. I want her to hear it in my voice. How much I need her. But she can't talk right now because she's getting ready for a date with the camp counselor. He showed up the night before and gave her a long gold chain with a T on it and told her he loves her. She isn't sure what she should wear. She loves Finn, she says, but she likes the camp counselor too. And when he showed up last night she was just wearing an old T-shirt and her hair was all a mess, but he liked the way she looked.

"He said I looked sexy," she says.

"Toy," I say, but it doesn't even sound like me. Can't she hear it?

They didn't have sex, she says. He didn't even try. They went up to her room and he took her guitar and played her a song he wrote for her. She curled her legs under her and pulled the T-shirt over her knees, so she looked, she says, sexy and innocent. And when the song was over he walked over to her, took her face in his hands and said he'll wait.

"As long as it takes," he said.

"Wait for what?" I say and my voice rises in frustration. "For what?" I say again. Because they've already had sex, she told me how it was, how romantic, and I want her to know what happened to me. I want to tell her about Sam.

But she ignores me. "Oh!" she says. "I know what I'll wear," and then she describes a soft summer dress. "With nothing underneath," she says and I interrupt.

"I have to talk to you, Toy," I say. "It's important. I have to see you."

And then she says, "Oh baby, are you OK?" Switching gears, just like that, because I think she likes it when I'm down.

"It doesn't matter," I say now because it doesn't. Because she's busy tonight, she has a date and by tomorrow it won't matter.

"I'll come over tomorrow," she says.

"OK," I say.

And she says, "OK." Then she says, "The pink dress. With nothing underneath."

"Yeah."

"But of course I'll wear the necklace."

"Of course," I say.

I go back to my apartment, pull open the heavy front door and walk up the familiar steps. My building has that smell that old apartments have and the hallway is dim. It's a Tuesday and it's quiet. Everyone's at work. I don't want to be alone anymore. I can't do this anymore. I make a plan. I'll take the bus to Toy's house and I'll be there when she comes back from her date. Her mom will let me in or I'll use the key from under the mat. I'll take the 38, the express bus, but it stops running soon, so I have to hurry.

I still smell like sex. In the mirror I'm flushed and feverish looking and I can see what Sam's mom saw when she looked at me. Her disappointment. I can never go back there, I think, and I want to just get on a bus and leave town. Go to Seattle like Angel. Or somewhere else. San Francisco. New York. Start all over. I put on jeans under my dress and pile on T-shirts and a sweatshirt because now I really do feel feverish and I'm sweating but I'm cold too. I pull the door shut. It's getting dark and I walk fast, swinging my arms to keep from crying.

The bus is empty and I rock my head against the glass and see my own wavering reflection. I keep picturing the T on a long gold chain that the camp counselor gave Toy. Real gold, she said. And I picture his hand on the side of her cheek and his gaze. Why does everyone treat her like a virgin when she's not? I picture her looking at him, her upturned face. I know how she poses so the light hits her perfectly. I know how she practices.

Everything is familiar once we reach the suburbs. I know every turn of every curved road. The way the houses settle back behind the trees. The long driveways and manicured lawns. When we get to Toy's stop the bus heaves to a standstill.

"Looks like I'm all alone now," the bus driver says when I get off.

I'm running a little and out of breath by the time I get down the street and around the corner to Toy's house. It's lit up from the inside. I'm shivering under my layers and ready to jump out of my skin. I feel like an idiot. Sam's family was never my family, I think, and I draw the big sweatshirt around me and put the hood up. I had no mother, I tell myself. I had no father. But now what? I knock on the door but nobody answers. I let myself in. I can hear the television from the master bedroom and I can picture Toy's mom asleep in front of it.

"It's me, Anna," I call and go to help myself to a soda from the refrigerator. Toy's mom is standing in the kitchen and she has some kind of piece of meat in her hands, like a chicken breast, dipped in flour and there's flour all over the counter and the front of her bathrobe.

"Hi," I say, worried that I startled her, but then she looks at me and I know I haven't at all. In the middle of the counter is her wineglass, the one she always uses, covered in sticky white fingerprints.

"Anna," she says and a smile attaches itself to her face but her eyes roam around me as though she knows I don't like looking at her directly. "I'm making dinner for Toy and me," she says, waving the piece of meat and

I know that later, after it's forgotten on the counter, Toy will have to throw it away.

"Toy's not here," I start to stay, but instead I turn and head up the carpeted stairs.

# the necklace

She's standing in front of the mirror when I walk in and when she turns it's as if she doesn't know who I am. She looks me over slowly like it's taking her a minute to place me.

"What are you wearing?" she says. I move closer to her so that our reflections are framed together in the mirror. It looks like I'm wearing everything I own. Like I'm running away from home.

"What are you doing here?" she says.

"What are you doing here?" I say. And then we don't say anything.

She's wearing an old T-shirt and her hair's all a mess. She stands next to me and I peel off some layers. The big sweatshirt and then a long-sleeved T-shirt.

"What's wrong with you?" she says. We're both staring into the mirror, into each other's eyes and I'm waiting for her to say it. But she won't say it. There's no necklace. So I say it.

"There's no necklace," I say and she's still looking at me in the mirror and then in a flash I understand. There's no camp counselor.

"Toy," I start. Her gaze is steady and defiant. And then I know. There's no Seth. There's no Finn.

# upside down

break her gaze. My sweatshirt is still in my hand. Toy's room is frilly and girly and spinning around us and I lock my eyes back on Toy's and look for my reflection there. Toy's stories weave around me and I think about all the times I wished that Seth was touching me like he touched her.

And collapsing. That first day in the Salvation Army, both of us framed in the mirror and how I wanted what she had. A boyfriend, she'd said. And what I'd felt. I'd wanted Joey to come back. I'd wanted Todd to show up and say it was all a mistake.

I'd wanted my story to make sense.

I'm sick. And I want to laugh. And I want to hurt her and I keep looking at her and I know, in a fractured second, that she's been hurt before.

Toy has a story too, I know suddenly, but I have no idea what it is.

And I can't remember why I came here tonight. Why am I here? It would be better if I didn't know. If it went back to the tell-me-again times. If I could go back to when I believed her. To when I thought she had every-thing. I look at the picture taped to the wall beside her bed. The one of her upside down like she's falling right out of the sky.

And it's like I can't even tell what's real anymore.

# after toy

I leave. I just walk out. I pass by Toy's mom's bedroom door and I wait for Toy to come after me but she doesn't. I imagine she runs after me and I turn around to face her. I'd wanted what she had.

"I couldn't figure out," I'd say, "why the boys in my life were nothing like the boys in yours."

When I get back to the city, the apartment is empty. I don't remember falling asleep.

# after sam

It's bright and hot. I call in sick to work and go to Little Birds cafe. It doesn't take long to meet a boy and right away he touches me. Reaches right across the table with two fingers and touches my cheek. Then he moves a piece of hair out of my eyes.

"Let's get out of here," he says.

I don't think about Sam. I don't think about Toy. I follow the boy to the corner where we buy a bottle of rum. The guy behind the counter doesn't even ask how old we are. We buy some soda and the boy sends me back to the cafe for two cups. I ask the girl with the dreadlocks to fill them with ice.

When I come out, he's waiting on the corner, past the liquor store, leaning against a mailbox with a brown paper bag in one hand. He's looking right at me, squinting against the sun. I don't need Toy, I think, and I hold up the cups so he can see them. He squints. He drapes one arm over my shoulders and I follow him down to the fountain. The one I passed yesterday on the way to Sam's house.

Just yesterday, I think.

It's the hottest day of summer, but a heavy canopy of green shades the city. We sit under a tree where the dirt is tamped down and we're out of sight. I take a good look at the boy but he doesn't look like anything special. I look at my legs in shorts. They're brown and kind of long and I like looking at them. I dig the heels of my sneakers into the dirt and roll my thighs back and forth. The boy pours two drinks, first the rum and then the Coke, right up to the rim. He hands one to me, spilling it on my legs. I take a big swallow, real fast. It's mostly rum. I lift up the cup and tap it against his.

"Cheers," I say. Already I'm narrating the story to myself. How I met this boy and how we got drunk together next to the roaring fountain.

He doesn't say anything, but leans back on one elbow and drinks. The fountain is so loud and I think maybe that's why we're not talking. The water flashes over concrete and brick. I take another swallow and then another.

Another and then another. It's hot, even in the shade. I think we should be saying something, but the boy leans back, eyes closed, so I just look at him. There's nothing familiar about him. My thigh leaning against his thigh. A stranger.

He catches me looking.

He pulls me down and pushes his mouth against mine, opening my mouth with his tongue. I spill my drink and he doesn't seem to care until it rolls down the dirt to his jeans and then he swears a little, but doesn't let go of me. I'm dizzy and roll onto my back, looking up through the branches at the hot cloudless sky. He rolls over so he's above me, leaning on one arm and kissing me. He's feeling around my chest with his other hand and I close my eyes and lay back against the ground. My feet splay open and I can picture us as if I were just someone walking by. Two kids in the bushes, in a city park, in the middle of the day.

I picture my mom walking by with her new boyfriend and him saying, "Her? That's your daughter?"

And then I picture Sam's mom walking by and seeing me. "Anna," she'd say. "Is that you?"

I push the boy back with one hand and his drink spills and he swears again. I push myself up so I'm sitting and I have to blink because it's so bright even in the shade. I take a big swallow and then another. It makes me feel less dizzy somehow, but more so too. I pull my knees up and together. I brush the dirt off my shoulders and look out at the crashing water.

Sam's mom would say, "Come on Anna, let's talk."

I'm having a long conversation with Sam's mom in my head and I feel the cringing burn of being caught with Sam. I'm apologizing and I can almost feel her touching my arm. "I'm sorry," I say, my eyes getting wet, and I picture myself stopping and turning to face her because I want so much for her to understand how I feel. I know this story. I know what comes next.

"You don't have to do this," I picture her saying and I don't know if she's talking about the boy. Or all of this. The fountain winks at me in the strong sunlight.

The boy refills my cup and I drink. School's let out and the park fills with kids. One little boy runs right up to edge of the fountain and wobbles there, about to pitch forward into the deepest end. But he falls backward instead and pulls off his shoes and socks as if the fountain can't possibly wait another second. The children's voices mix with the tinny sound of the water and the adults gather in the shade. At first they don't notice me and the boy drinking out of paper cups, but when they do, they take their kids and move to the far side of the park.

It's so hot. I drink from my cup. I no longer want Sam's mom to walk past. My T-shirt is damp and heavy and I'm wet where my skin folds, on my belly and under my breasts. The boy's focused on drinking and my vision has narrowed so that when I look at him I can't see anything else and when I look back at the fountain it's ringed by darkness.

I know what I need to do. I need to get in that fountain. I have an idea of how I'll look, sitting by the edge, trailing my fingers in the water with bits of light on my face. I pull off my sneakers and grab the side of the tree to pull myself up. I tug on the boy and try and pull him up too, but he shrugs me off. It takes three tries and I'm up. I look over the fountain and take aim. I concentrate on getting over to the spot where the little boy had been.

I make it. I fall heavily, scrape my calf and sit on the edge dangling my legs in the water. It's cold and clear and I can see coins in the bottom. And I think that's where the sound comes from, because the fountain sounds like coins poured down a stone chute. I'm getting wet and I'm covered in goose bumps and I have everything. Everything. All I need in this moment is this boy. Any boy.

I push away thoughts like ghosts. Scooping up water in my hand and pouring it over my bare legs. I had no father, I say. I had no mother. And then you came along and everything changed.

I turn and point at the boy, but he isn't there. I lean back against the warm concrete and stare up at the sky. Then I see he's standing over me, a shadow against the sun. I don't remember his name.

"Get up," he says and I squint at him. He struggles to pull me up. I forget and start remembering everything to tell Toy later. Then I remember. I lean against the boy.

"Let's go to your place," he says. But it's impossible to stand. I'm holding the boy and he's holding me. We hold onto anything we can. We walk a few feet and then lean against a lamppost, a mailbox, a bench. It's so hot. I've forgotten my shoes and the cement burns my feet. The sidewalk fills with people on their way home from work. They tower above us, walking fast. I lean over and throw up next to a fire hydrant. The boy holds a fistful of my shirt. I wipe my mouth with the back of my hand and stand up. I lead the boy through the park blocks and past the Safeway to the front door of my building.

The boy is holding onto my shirt with both fists and leaning against me and I reach out one hand and lean us both against the heavy brick wall. I imagine Sam waiting for me on my front steps. I look at myself with his eyes. The boy's hand is on my breast and there's vomit on the front of my T-shirt. I'm barefoot.

The boy pulls the bottle of rum out of the brown paper sack and drinks. He hands it to me and I drink too. I take him up the stairs, two flights to my apartment. I unlock the door and head straight back to the kitchen. I'll make some coffee, I think. I met a boy and took him home, I rehearse to tell Toy. I wash two coffee cups, the yellow and the blue. I pour coffee into the filter and fill the machine with water. I walk back into the front room.

The boy is standing in the center of the room, turning around and looking at the pictures of girls taped to my wall.

"Is this what you want," he says. "You want to look like some slut?"

# slut

I'm a slut before I ever touch a penis. Before I ever have sex. The space between Desmond Dreyfus with his damp palm over my breast while Carl Drier and Michael Cox watch to my mouth around Joey Sugimoto's penis is very short. The girl I am now, at sixteen, was always present. She haunted the twelve-year-old me.

# in the doorway

I look at the boy. At his unwashed hair and the way his eyes narrow, but won't focus. I take him by the wrist and with one hand on his shoulder, I angle him out the door.

"Hey," he says and we're standing in the doorway with him mostly outside and me mostly inside. I push the bottle of rum into his palm. "What?" he says, confused. "You want to be alone?" But I don't answer.

I shut the door behind him.

# after the boy

And then I'm alone again in the empty apartment. I stand at the door listening to the blood rush in my head. Picturing the boy weaving down the hall and down the stairs. I make my way to the bathroom and retch until I can't anymore. Until there's nothing left.

I hug my arms tight around me and rest my head against the tub. Next to the mirror is a picture of two girls, hands clasped, surrounded by a busy market. They aren't looking at each other but connected, their hands held tight.

I think about Toy. I dismantle every story she told me. Every glance, every touch, every word. Every boy. An hour passes and the drumming in my head slows. I repeat Toy's stories to myself and now all I see are ragged seams. All the parts that didn't make sense. She's never had a Sam walk her to her door and kiss her good night. Or take off his jacket and cover her shoulders with it. She's never been touched by a boy who knows what love looks like. I picture Sam's parents, his mom resting her hand in the center of his dad's back and the way his dad leans back against her. How would Toy know what that looks like?

Her stories are just guesses.

I fall asleep here, against the tub, but maybe just for a minute, because it's still light out. And then I get up, shaking out my legs, and drink the coffee I'd made earlier. The cream curdles in my cup.

# in the kitchen

Toy's pile of pictures are still in a stack on the table, the bruised girl on top. I listen to the familiar noises of my apartment and I almost feel good again. The olive oil I bought is in a little drizzler that Sam's mom gave me, sitting on an antique plate with orange flowers and gold trim. My apron hangs next to the refrigerator from a little hook that I screwed in myself. There's a bowl of oranges on the counter. I look at the picture, black-and-white, of the family tumbling out of a summer home. I look at it like I always do, eyes resting on the girl who's my age, but this time I see something different. She's leaning back and looking up and she's relaxed. Confident. She knows where she belongs. Her family knows her, they know things about her—the things that make her crazy, the ways to tease her, how quickly her skin turns red in the sun. I think about dinner at Sam's house. Sam's sister, Em, setting the table and teasing me, like I belonged there. Sam's dad giving me the chicken leg, because he knows it's my favorite. I open my eyes wide against the late-afternoon light and circle my hands against the warm coffee cup.

# family

The difference is I can see them all here. My family. My mom and Toy. And I can see Sam and his family. All packed into my little apartment, sharing chairs and sitting on the floor. Making do with the plates and silverware and cups that I have. Eating together. The difference is I don't want to go anywhere. Not Seattle. Not back to the suburbs or back to high school. Or back. I want to go forward and I don't have to go anywhere to do it. My family is here. I don't have to do it alone.

# tell me again

In the tell-me-again times, my mom let me sleep in her bed. Her bed is a raft on the ocean. It's a cloud, a forest, a spaceship, a cocoon we share. I stretch out big as I can, a five-pointed star, and she bundles me back up in her arms. When I wake I'm tangled in her hair.

"Tell me again," I say and she tells me again how she wanted me more than anything.

"More than anything in the world," she says, "I wanted a little girl."

"Tell me again," I say.

"I was all alone," she says. "And then I had you."


Now I can hear how much is missing from this story.

# my story

I'm sober now and stiff and the apartment smells like burnt coffee. I run a bath and submerge. A bath is like a chance to do it all over again. My hair fans out from my face and I float with my eyes closed. This is all of me, I think. And it means something different now.

She had me, but it didn't make her any less alone. And the boyfriends and the husbands and the houses, they don't make her any less alone either. Maybe the stories she tells herself are no truer than Toy's.

Toy and my mom haven't abandoned me, I think. They need me.

"You're strong," Sam's mom had said. "You can do anything."

"So strong," my mom had said.

You don't have to do this alone, I want to tell Toy. You're not alone, I want to tell my mom. I'm lying in the bath and saying the words out loud. And I picture the scar on Toy's collarbone and the sound of her voice when she takes the phone away from her mom. The empty swimming pool behind her house, the rotting rhododendrons. Her mom's faded dresses.

I think about the night of the abortion. Toy and my mom together. Taking care of me. I sit up and hook my legs over the side of the tub. I think about Sam.

Maybe I'm the lucky one, I think.

And I think about me and my mom and Toy and her mom and our missing fathers. It all swirls around me and I can't just stay here. I need to do something. I need to say something. I need to tell Toy. I need to tell my mom. I need them to know that I know. And I have to hear that Sam's OK. And his mom. I want his mom to know—

What?

They're my family. And the stories we tell ourselves are not the only stories. Our story, I think, could start here.

I get out and wrap myself in a towel. In the mirror, I look like myself. I stretch and the girl in the mirror stretches too.

I'm going to find them and tell them, I think, and I put on my favorite jeans and a striped T-shirt and I tuck my hair behind my ears. I pull on my sneakers over bare feet and grab my keys and run out of the apartment, down the hall, taking two steps at a time.

# our story

When I finally make my way to Sam's house, it's dusk and the first stars are poking through the heavy sky.

I ring the bell, before anything else, and hear footsteps, light ones, and it's Em who opens the door. She smiles her sunny, easy smile and hugs me around my waist.

"Anna. Oh!" And then she turns around and yells, "It's Anna." She turns back to me and says in a whisper, "My mom was so worried about you."


Later, Sam walks me home and we hold hands. We don't talk. It's dark, but it's a kind of summer dark where the sky is still light. When we turn onto my street, Sam points.

"What's that?" he says.

There's a figure sitting, huddled on my steps. We step closer and then I stop. It's the boy from the fountain. The boy who called me a slut.

I grip Sam's hand in mine and step forward, ready to

send the boy away again. Ready to do whatever it takes. I walk faster. The figure sits up for a second and then settles back down. It's not a boy at all.

It's Toy. She hugs her knees and rests her head against her forearms. I pull Sam along by the hand.

"Come on," I say. "There's someone I want you to meet."

# acknowledgments

For Marnie and Lucy, I love you. I'm grateful to Sarah Davies, who saw to the heart of the thing. For my editor, Jennifer Weis, who took a chance on Anna's story. And to Mollie Traver and the team at St. Martin's Press, thank you for everything. Special thanks to Ally Hack. And love to Ginger and Holly. And to Clara Azulay, Elana K. Arnold, Matthew Florence, Vanessa Hua, Jen Larkin, Wendy MacNaughton, Heather Malcom, Kathleen Miller, Sophie Nunberg, Caroline Paul, and Somlynn Rorie. Thanks to Jonathan D. Gray. And Jonathan Segol. And to 826 Valencia. Love to my dad and Lidia. And to David. For Pam Houston for believing in language and in stories and in this story. Thanks to Lucy Corin and Lynn Freed for their generosity. Thanks to Headlands Center for the Arts, the Community of Writers, NY Summer Writers Institute, SCBWI, and the University of California, Davis, for the encouragement and support. To Rick Moody, for reminding me to be patient, and to Francesca Lia Block who, like me, believes in girls.

"With her expected wit and humor, Lorna Seilstad has penned another winner. You'll be captivated by the characters and history in *The Ride of Her Life*. Hang on and enjoy—this book is truly a fun ride."

—**Judith Miller**, bestselling author of the Daughters of Amana series

"Buckle up, it's going to be a fun ride! With a sparkle of humor, heart-pumping romance, and a writing style that is fresh, fun, and addictive, Lorna Seilstad takes you on *The Ride of Her Life*—and yours—along the fun-filled shores of 1906 Lake Manawa."

—**Julie Lessman**, award-winning author of the Daughters of Boston and the Winds of Change series

Prais

"Lorna Seilstad pulled [me into] Lake Manawa with the [...] of summer days. But th[...] made the book great. This needs to be everyone's first choice for a vacation read, or if you just want to open the pages of a book and be transported from your recliner to the beach."

—**Mary Connealy**, author of *Doctor in Petticoats* [and] *Wrangler in Petticoats*

Prai[se]

"*A Great Catch* weave[s ...] truths into a delicious s[...] a fun, relaxing read! I'[...]

—**Laura Fra**[nk ...]

"*A Great Catch* is a [...] invigorating as lemon[...] a woman's relationsh[ip ...] in her life—while ma[...] running to get in on t[...]

—**Sarah** [...]

# Books by Lorna Seilstad

LAKE MANAWA SUMMERS

*Making Waves*
*A Great Catch*
*The Ride of Her Life*